"Reminiscent of Raymond Chandler's *The Big Sleep*."

—*Capital Times*

"Larsen's novel comes to us in the guise of a gripping crime story. At the same time it is a provocative critique of the world's obsession with technology and blind faith in progress."

—*Berliner Morgenpost*

"A dark psychological thriller . . . A tight, suspenseful plot."

—*Fort Lauderdale Sun-Sentinel*

"A skillfully crafted, thoughtful, and evocative novel that calls to mind a winning mixture of Michael Crichton's technology-laced plots and Thomas Harris's tormented characters."

—*Booklist*

"Fast-moving."

—*Kirkus Reviews*

Uncertainty

Michael Larsen

Uncertainty A NOVEL

Translated from the Danish by
Lone Thygesen Blecher and George Blecher

Fawcett Columbine
The Ballantine Publishing Group • New York

A Fawcett Columbine Book
Published by The Ballantine Publishing Group

This is a translation of UDEN SIKKER VIDEN.

This is a work of fiction. All the names, characters, organizations, and events portrayed in this book are either the products of the author's imagination or are used fictitiously for verisimiltude. Any resemblance to any organization or any actual person, living or dead, is unintended.

http://www.randomhouse.com

Library of Congress Catalog Card Number: 97-90646

ISBN: 0-449-91236-1

This edition published by arrangement with Harcourt Brace & Company.

Cover design by David Stevenson
Cover image based on a photo © Nick Dolding/Tony Stone Images

Manufactured in the United States of America

First Ballantine Books Edition: February 1998

10 9 8 7 6 5 4 3 2 1

Uncertainty

Chapter One

Except for a corner of the bedding that's nicked off, the bed is as white and taut as a soft down coffin. Every night a small square appears like magic on the pillow. Peppermint chocolate in silver foil, cooled below the melting point. Is it meant to be eaten before or after you brush your teeth? I've never quite understood that piece of chocolate.

The flowers in the vases have a freshness that seems almost unreal. Sweet-smelling and bursting with green juices, they are hyacinths and squeaky-leafed, yellow tulips: through the vases the water shines crystal clear like chrome or sun-splintered rain.

No doubt about it: the photograph was taken here. Not in this exact room, but in one of the many rooms of the hotel. The mirror and the texture of the dusty crimson wallpaper in the background give it away. Even with the two figures in close-up, you can make out the tiny upholstered cushions which, like a fingerprint, link the wall in the photo with a wall in one of the rooms. The colors change from floor to floor. On the fifth the wallpaper's a subdued yellow, as in the photo. That's where it was taken.

Her face is strangely contorted. Contorted with pleasure. As he holds her wrist tightly, she pushes herself backward against him, her fists clenched. The mirror, the wallpaper, the sweat on their bodies are all visible.

I can't keep my eyes off the picture. I keep staring at it even though it makes me gag. The bed they're lying on is rumpled, the sheets pulled askew: a pillow's been pushed between her legs. The graininess of the picture makes it even smuttier.

This woman—who wanders through my dreams like a ghost suspended in time, whose fluttering lashes I can still feel against my neck like a frightened butterfly—flings her body backward as if letting herself be rammed by a pole, devouring it from below. At the moment they took the picture, her head jerked backward, as if she either died or came.

I don't know him. I'm guessing the name on the note is his, but I'm not sure. And what about her? I ought to know her, but I'm not sure I do. I'm guessing.

In my dreams her face is still young. She's still cool, round, and soft, with hands made only for caressing. Can I connect her to the woman in the picture? I find it difficult. Maybe it's the short hair. When I saw her last, it was long and blond. In the letter Marianne sent with the photo, she said that Monique also dyed it after she'd had it cut.

Outside my door the hallways are quiet. Distant sounds penetrate the womblike security as through a light sleep. At night, when they bring up silver platters and sparkling decanters, the waiters in their white jackets and black, razor-creased pants speak in the hushed voices of discreet lovers. The street far below is silent.

Though the sound of the bell on the ornate elevator can't be completely muffled, the massive mahogany door to my room, a room hissing with artificially cooled air, makes even that sound almost imperceptible. Occasionally someone pushes messages and letters under the door, but the only sound they make is a slight rustle and a white whisper across the carpet. They're usually from Solker. He worries about my expenses.

After the descent in the elevator, which leaves a faint deafness and a slight sense of exhaustion, one steps into the lobby. It's quiet there too. In the tall-pillared silence, the leather feet of business people across the deep-pile carpets make no sound at all. You'd need microphones to pick up conversations, curiously dead and intimate. Trails in the carpet reveal the unheard bustle, while invisible servants constantly erase and sweep away the shadows and dust.

Beneath the cathedrallike dome in the front hall, the men seem clean, well-groomed, and odorless, and the pomade in their short, black hair gleams wetly like dew from a bath. Their colorful silk ties give them an aura of boyish innocence, and the thought of their multimillion-dollar deals seems incongruous. Around the women swirl invisible, dizzying clouds of fragrance. Most wear high-necked, tailored, solid-colored suits; others wear dresses, with only the slits in their skirts allowing them to move. They could be young wives, girlfriends, or colleagues: you can't tell. They might also be bought women. Their soft shoulders are large and square; as they walk, their gliding, pointy footsteps seem to be squashing something underfoot. They look like colorful carnivores, their faces white with smiles and their shiny lips blood red, almost dripping.

There's a majestic stylishness in the hotel corridors. Everything warm pastels asleep in English red, crimsons, pale sandy yellow, and a single cold color which manages to make the bathroom larger and the water warmer—a cool green echoed in the detailing of the white towels and washcloths and in the wrappers of the hotel soap bars.

The day I arrived, they wanted to know which newspapers I wanted delivered to my room with my breakfast. But of course they didn't have any from Denmark.

The tips I give young Stuart, Louis, and the others are the only money that passes between us. Everything else is done by credit card. Everyone's polite and smiling, almost homosexually friendly. No one recognizes the man in my photograph.

"And I would have remembered *her*," says Stuart.

"But I know she was here!"

Stuart shakes his head. "I don't remember."

He doesn't comment on the photo, asks no questions. Merely regrets not being able to help.

I can ring for Stuart—or any of the others—at any time of day or night. I can have my clothes cleaned or washed. When I want a car, I just press a button. If I have no special food requests, I can call down for one of the daily specials. The staff are like shadows in my life. Only once do I have to call for something I can't find in the minibar. I can press a button to get a massage, to have the fifth-floor pool opened or my shoes polished or pants pressed.

And I can call when I run out of pills; the hotel doctor takes care of the rest. All they need is the prescription, and only the first time.

"Bad dreams again, sir?"

"No dreams at all."

As he stands in the doorway in his white gloves and beige tasseled uniform, the young man from Reception looks like a circus ringmaster.

"It's important that you call home."

I open the discreetly folded letter. It's from Solker. "Stars! We want stars! Otherwise you'll have to pay for the hotel yourself. How about Cher?"

"Also, would you please call Louis in room service?" the young man says. I hand him some money and go back inside to turn on the computer. "Something's on the way," I write. Then I call room service.

"Hello, Mr. Molberg," says Louis. "I have good news. Mr. Nicholson just arrived."

"Thank you, Louis. Where can I find him?"

"Probably by the pool, sir."

"Thank you, Louis."

"My pleasure, sir."

I take a Perrier from the minibar and swallow a couple of Dexedrines. Then I blow off some steam by adding to Solker's message on the screen: "Something's on the way—something big." I pace around the room for a while before I take a Thorazine to take myself down a few notches.

I know that all I have to do is ask Louis—Louis knows everything about Hollywood—but I send off a message to Stella in Records to get the latest on Nicholson. I leave the modem open.

Sitting down and smoking a cigarette, I can feel the Dexedrines kicking in.

Am I going to have trouble with Borris? Should I call and tell him? But Solker knows what I'm after, and I still get furious when I think of how little help Borris gave me before I left. "Call these," he said with his head buried in a book, and gave me, among others, the names of Tom Cruise's and Cher's agents. It was nice of him to help me out, I thought, until I found the same book in all the shops on Sunset Boulevard. Naively I'd thought that agents were there to help you contact their clients; actually they're there to prevent it. "Call us when you get here," I kept hearing over and over. Meanwhile Solker was pumping me about the appointments I'd made so far. "We're not going to pay if you don't get anything," he said. I assured him that all was well, that all I had to do was call when I arrived. And all along, I imagine, Jan Borris was having a good laugh at my expense. When I got to Los Angeles, I had no trouble picturing him thinking: LA's a big city, Molberg's probably still looking for the hotel. After God knows how many calls to Cher's agent, I gave up. Mine was now the leading paper in Europe, but that didn't help.

"Enough already. Cher's sick, can't you understand that? She's having an operation."

"You mean an alteration?" And I banged down the receiver.

Tom Cruise also suddenly got sick. That night I saw him drive off with Nicole Kidman from La Dôme after some party or other.

I pack a small bag with the basics: a notepad, from which I tear a few pages and sprinkle them into the bag, and a bunch of pens, one of which I stick in my bathing trunks to be on the safe side. The tape recorder I don't include: it's too risky. No problem about a camera: everyone here has one. Cigarettes, take lots of cigarettes: he smokes a lot. I put on a T-shirt and a pair of loose, long pants over my bathing suit; the white robe from the bathroom I hang over my arm.

The sun is shining on the white-clad pool waiters, and the water clucks and gurgles, its edges sending off triangular flashes of light. A solitary splash from a guest is the only sound other than the dry rustle from the palm leaves in the light breeze. Downtown skyscrapers in the distant reddish haze line the horizon.

There's no sign of Nicholson.

I lie down and feel the sun and the Thorazines relaxing my body. I order iced tea from one of the waiters and light a cigarette while I wonder which chair he'll choose. I regret not having asked Louis if Mr. Nicholson has a regular spot, if he comes here often—and why he comes. As far as I recall, he lives in a mansion in the Hollywood hills. Maybe it has to do with a movie. Or a press conference. Or some junket, as Borris likes to call them.

I put out my cigarette and light a new one; he may be the type who likes to smoke other people's cigarettes.

Just after noon he turns up, wearing a bathrobe, a white towel around his neck. He grins and hesitates for a moment on the steps leading down to the pool. Apparently he has no regular spot. The pool waiter hurries him to a lounge chair not far from mine. I go over and over this scene in my mind and memorize every word Mr. Nicholson and the waiter say, knowing well that it may be all I'll get.

"And no phones—unless it's about a movie," he tells the waiters, grinning, and they laugh heartily, for of course those will be the only calls. There are many: the phone rings incessantly, keeping the waiters jogging back and forth. Mr. Nicholson nods to me politely as he sits on his lounger. Then he lies down.

After he's settled in, I make my first trip to the bathroom. I've managed to smuggle a few slips of paper into my trunks, and I make my first notes, using the toilet stall to write on. Tomorrow I'll get some postcards, so he'll think I'm just writing home. Otherwise I'll have to keep making notes in the bathroom.

Later in the afternoon, Mr. Nicholson retreats under the shade of an umbrella. I've been to the bathroom several times, and I'm afraid he is becoming suspicious. We still haven't exchanged a word, and by now there are more people at the pool; perhaps the rumor of his presence has got around.

"It's a great movie," he says to one of the waiters, giving him an autograph. "Incredible special effects. You won't believe it."

He's reading a book as one of the waiters approaches with the telephone. He's about to get up, but the waiter walks past and comes to me.

It's Solker.

"How big is it?"

I look at Mr. Nicholson, who smiles. I smile back.

"Big," I say. Considering all the calls Mr. Nicholson has had today, it's not likely that he's impressed by mine. But this gives me a cover. The fact that a newspaper is calling isn't obvious. Around here people think Business.

"*How* big?" Solker asks.

I look at Mr. Nicholson.

"Very big."

When I hang up, Mr. Nicholson looks up from his book.

"Business?" he says.

"Can't even keep it out of the cabanas," I sigh.

"Hmmm." He smiles again. "I like that. Mind if I use it some day?"

"Be my guest."

That evening in the lobby, I see Mr. Nicholson and his wife trailed by photographers. Maybe they, too, tasted the warm foie gras in the hotel restaurant and decided to eat out. Whoever heard of heating foie gras?

"It's a shame you won't be here when it opens," Louis says. "Incredible special effects."

"Yes, that's what Nicholson says."

That night in the hotel restaurant, I see the flight attendant for the first time. Still in her uniform, she's eating alone; she probably just arrived. Our eyes meet. She smiles. Her mouth is red and fruitlike. When no one's looking, she licks it with her tongue. I smile back. The resemblance is incredible.

Around noon the next day, Mr. Nicholson is back at the pool. But he doesn't want to be photographed.

"Not here," he says. "God forbid people should think I lie around not doing anything. In a few weeks I'll have the TV and magazines after me. The same questions day in and day out."

Most of my high from having got the better of Borris evaporates when I think of the computer and the pile of notes that have to be written up and sent back home. I have more important things on my mind: the little crumpled note from Monique and the picture Marianne sent. She wrote that it must have been taken the last week of March, when Monique had her hair cut. I have bits and pieces, but nothing really connects. Still, he has to be the one who belongs to the name Monique wrote on the note.

I write a few postcards, but continue making notes in the bathroom; too many postcards would seem improbable.

"Again?" he asks incredulously when I get up to go.

"Bladder," I say.

"Hell of a bladder," he replies.

Later that afternoon, we're standing across from each other in the pool when he begins to philosophize about his career. At some point he asks me what I do. I tell him I'm "in paper."

I realize how hard it is to get a conversation going without sounding inquisitive.

The water gurgles around us.

"What about money? You must have made millions," I say.

He smiles.

"Money?" he says. "Money's okay—when you can see it on the screen. And you can in my new film. When I think about what those guys can do today. Jesus, I play myself at thirty."

I wonder how they managed that, but stop myself from asking when I can't think of a polite way to say it. Anyway, Hollywood lives on makeup.

"Money? It brings problems you never had before. The only difference is that now you can buy your way out of them. That's how I look at money: it buys you out of problems you never used to have."

"I like that," I say. "Mind if I use it someday?"

He grins, the famous grin.

"Be my guest."

I sit down to write the interview. A few minutes after it's written and sent, Solker calls.

"Nicholson," he says admiringly. "How did you get him?"

"Ask Borris."

"Jan is okay."

"Jan is an idiot."

"What do you mean?"

I don't elaborate. In principle people aren't interested in how things happen, as long as they happen. They couldn't care less for explanations and despise apologies. They hate a lot of talk, prefer their information in the form of headlines, and get a far-away look in their eyes when confronted with complaints. Unless, that is, you're a star like Mr. Nicholson.

"What about pictures?" Solker says.

"He doesn't want them."

"You know you can always call AP."

"He doesn't want them."

"I'm just telling you. He's got good things to say," Solker says.

"Of course."

"Did he really say them?"

"What do you think?"

Solker doesn't ask any more questions. Like all reporters, he knows that the more you ask about a story, the smaller it gets, until it disappears.

A while later, I call Barbra at the *Los Angeles Times* archives, but she hasn't found anything for me.

"You said the name was Pascal? Jack Roth Pascal?"

"Yes."

"I'm afraid he's not in here. I could try some of the other databases."

"Never mind, Barbra. Thanks anyway."

I sit for a few moments with a Unisom in my hand, trying to decide if it's turquoise or aqua. Then I pick up the receiver and call Marianne. No answer. While I wait with the receiver on my cheek, I break the little tablet in half and swallow both halves, then wash them down with straight whiskey. When the signal dies, I hang up.

I bring along the photograph when I leave the room and walk to the elevator. The sand in the pedestaled ashtrays is clean and raked into elegant patterns. On the fifth floor the wallpaper is a light ochre, as in the picture. I turn the corner, look cautiously in both directions—no one around—and follow the numbers to room 505. You feel strangely guilty and vulnerable in a hotel corridor where you have no business and no key to any of the rooms; after all, letting yourself in and out of a room is the only thing to do in a hotel corridor. When I reach room 505, all I can think of doing is to pass it and continue down the hall. As I pass, I listen for sounds but hear nothing.

When the elevator bell rings, I spot an emergency exit and take a few quick steps across the deep-pile carpet, turn, and press myself against the door. A woman is walking in my direction. Feeling like an idiot, I squeeze against the exit; there are more rooms farther down the corridor, and I pray that she'll stop at a door before reaching my hiding place. If she doesn't, I have no idea what I'll say.

She knocks on a door not far from where I'm standing. It opens and shuts behind her. Not a word is said. To be on the safe side, I stay where I am a few moments before stepping out.

After the first few steps, I feel safe again. Now I'm just another guest who's walked out of a room and is on his way to the elevator. All the tension's gone.

As I pass the various rooms, I listen for signs of life behind the doors, but there's nothing to hear. Nothing in room 505 either. Maybe that's the room she entered. I try—without success—to conjure up a picture of the woman I only caught a glimpse of. All I see is hair—long, blond, fluttering hair—and a dress that flapped around her. Not a uniform. But she could have changed clothes. I'm almost sure it was the flight attendant from the restaurant.

Back in my room, I lie on my bed and wait for the pill to kick in. Nothing. I call Marianne again. No answer.

The next morning, I wake up sitting in my chair with the receiver dangling down my back.

————

One evening before dinner, I grab the concierge, give him the name Monique Milazar, and ask him to find it in the computer records from March. But he won't be bribed.

"I'm sorry, sir, but you must understand that we can't give out that kind of privileged information. If I made an exception, it would mean that anyone at all could get information about any of the guests in the hotel."

"What about Jack Pascal? Jack Roth Pascal?"

He looks at me unblinkingly. "That includes information about you. How would you like that?"

"I've had a minor nervous breakdown. I'm taking Thorazine and some antidepressants."

He looks at me calmly. "I wouldn't know anything about that."

As discreet as a bordello. I give up trying to bribe him; the lobby is full of harassed guests, and I have a feeling that at this moment he's impervious to everything.

I eat dinner in the hotel restaurant.

Shrimp with silky black eyes and crabs steamed in white wine. Sweet wines and the citrus taste of a palate-cleansing sorbet, a meal in itself. Roast beef with lingonberry sauce, sun-dried tomatoes, and slices of lime, bread that's soft and spongy and tastes of grain. A dessert cart and a platter overflowing with dusty-purple grapes and other fruits. Cheeses that melt like milk in your mouth. I take a picture of one especially gorgeous arrangement—the only picture I take. One of the headwaiter's arms gets in the picture.

There is a word to describe this: psychologists would call it an aberration. Even if it's an aberration in the world of psychology, which after all consists of nothing but aberrations, some aberrations are more normal than others. Maybe Dr. Phillip has a better word for it.

The weight of a silver fork can make a man tumble forward. The headwaiter with the big, stiff, broomlike mustache manages to get me out of the room quickly . What strikes me is how suddenly everything seems to have frozen in place. As another arm is placed under me, I can't even hear the rustle of the women's evening gowns made of pleated and puffed taffeta—not even the cascading sound of the tulle. One doesn't faint here; it just isn't done. But our psyches crack, like mosaics, long before our bodies start to buckle: everything goes black before my eyes.

Young Louis, who's only a few years younger than me, accompanies me to my room. But as he is about to call a doctor, I pant and point to the pill glass.

The path to my mental well-being lies like hidden codes in these little capsules and tablets. I feel almost moved by them: they never let me down. As dependable as the muscles in a sprained back, they step in, without fail, to support the weak points. The thought that they'll never be able completely to remove the pain makes me feel tender: it's as though they know it.

When I start to come around, I reach for my wallet. But Louis waves me off.

"There's no need for money."

It's the first time I've ever heard an American say that. I look up at him.

"The first public showing of a motion picture?" I ask.

He smiles. "The Brothers Lumière, 1895."

"Where?"

"Paris."

"Scott Fitzgerald?"

"Died at the age of forty-four in 1940. Wrote *The Great Gatsby*, and never really figured Hollywood out."

"I never will either, Louis."

I lie back on the bed. The others leave; only Louis stays.

"Thank you, Louis."

"Sir?"

"For Mr. Nicholson."

He smiles. "Don't mention it."

I reach for my wallet again and pull out a hundred-dollar bill. He takes it and then puts it on the bedside table.

"No, sir, what I meant was, don't mention it to anyone."

"I know, Louis. I know."

My head's heavy, and there's a dusty buzz of chemical synapses in my body.

As he's about to leave, I say, "I want to ask you a small favor. There's a Danish flight attendant staying here. I'd like to know when she checks out."

I don't even remember her name. But the next day at the breakfast buffet, a woman walks up to me, smiling, and invites me for a drink in her room. Her hair's pulled up tightly in a black column. I don't know her, I have never spoken to her before. Her eyes are dark and warm; in her loose, white summer dress she looks like a Greek goddess.

In her room I jokingly tell her that she should lie down so we can look into each other's eyes. This happens wordlessly. It's the first time I make love to a woman who's taller than me.

In the morning, she's gone. All that's left is an odd, low-grade melancholy and a faint, fading throb in my penis. Like a distended, expiring heart. Or a swollen finger. Like a conversation in an almost forgotten tongue.

The next morning, I share a table with an American. When I stand up, he sizes me up. On a long shot he hands me his card.

"If you ever need a divorce lawyer."

"You're too late," I say with a wilted little smile. "She just died."

Chapter Two

In the photograph her hair is short and blond, but I know her only with long hair, that's how I remember her. Maybe that's why Stuart and the others don't recognize her. And she dyed it at the end. I can't visualize it at all, but that's what Marianne wrote. Chestnut brown.

Later that morning, I call Marianne again. Finally she picks up.

"Where have you been?"

"Paris," she says. "I took a couple of extra days off."

"Where did you find it?"

"In the bookcase. In one of the books. She must have put it there."

She lights a cigarette. With the receiver in my hand, I walk around the room and pick up a pack of cigarettes. I get a handful of loose tobacco, then tap one out and light it.

"Where are you?" she says.

"Los Angeles."

"What are you doing there?"

"Working. Did you show it to anyone else?"

"No. But I thought you'd better see it right away."

I let a finger circle her face in the picture. A tiny gray leaf of ash whirls down and falls on her body; I blow it away.

"Who is he?" I ask.

"I don't know. I thought you might."

"Why did she cut it? It isn't becoming."

"She was bored with it."

"Marianne, was there someone else?"

"No."

"It sure looks like there was."

"There wasn't. I don't know who he is."

"There's always someone else when women suddenly start changing the way they look."

"Monique didn't need to change her looks."

I take a deep drag on the cigarette, then stub it out so hard the filter breaks.

"Does the name Jack Pascal mean anything to you? Jack Roth Pascal?"

"No. Listen, Martin, I'm sorry I sent it, but I didn't know what else to do."

"Take it easy. It's all right. Actually that's the reason I'm here."

"Do *you* know who he is?" she says.

"I think he's the man in the photograph."

"How do you know that?"

"I'm guessing."

A little later that day, Solker calls from Copenhagen.

"They're asking why we can't quote him directly," he says.

"It just wouldn't be a good idea."

"They say it weakens it a bit."

"Then quote him directly."

"Not if you didn't speak to him directly."

Of course I spoke to him, I explain. Solker says that Jan Borris doesn't like the fact that there aren't any pictures. Even though reporters live by the word, no one loves to worry about pictures more than they do. Without pictures, nothing.

"His agent doesn't want it. Just tell Borris that. He'll understand."

He doesn't comment any further. Just breathes heavily and changes the subject. "There's a message for you from Mimi at the front desk. Your bank called a couple of times. She has the number for you."

"Tell her I'll call her. Could you transfer me to Stella in Records?"

"Just a second," he says.

Stella hasn't found anything.

"But don't worry, Martin. If he's there, we'll find him," she says. "You did say Jack Roth Pascal. I've been thinking that if his family was English, then maybe Jack could really be Jacob. You know the way Americans Americanize."

"Good idea. Try it."

"And you really have nothing else?"

"No."

"It may take some time, Martin."

"It can take time," I say. "Just not a lot."

I log out and start to pack so that I'll be ready to leave when Louis calls. It goes quickly, and when I can't think of anything else to do, I turn on the TV. It's hard to relax.

In the hospital the doctors diagnosed the hollow, inner pain that I dull with Zantac as mourning, and the endless stream of thoughts that rush through my head at night, killing dreams that should give me ease, as unresolved anguish. Anyway, that's what they said.

As I lie sprawled on the bed, waves of thought keep rolling over me; it's a relief when I hear Louis gently tapping at the door.

"Evening, sir. Just checking the minibar." He walks soundlessly over to the half-empty cabinet.

"Another party?" he says, amazed.

I nod, and ask him to fill it up. When he's done, I slip him a folded five-dollar bill. He smiles and thanks me, then walks toward the door.

"Greta Garbo?" I say.

He turns, smiling. "1905."

"Her real name?"

"Gustafsson."

I smile. "Who's Jack Roth Pascal?"

He squints.

"Is he in films?"

"I don't know. I don't think so."

"Everyone here is in films."

I get up from the bed, take the photo from the desk, and show it to him.

"Is that him?" he asks. Just like the others I've shown the photo to, he doesn't miss a beat—in spite of what he sees. Apparently nothing the guests might decide to do, however weird, is considered objectionable.

"I don't know."

"Who is she?" he asks.

"Monique Milazar."

He shakes his head, repeats the name Jack Roth Pascal, then

shakes his head again. "The name seems familiar, but I don't recognize this guy." He shrugs and repeats the name on his way to the door.

"Don't worry about it," I tell him. "Your memory is terrific."

He turns. "Thank you, sir."

"What about the hotel records?"

"I'm afraid that can't be done, sir. They can tell if we go into the computer; we're not allowed to."

"Louis, I was just wondering. Would you ever consider selling information?"

"Sing like a bird, sir?"

"Why not?" I scratch my fingers together. "Information. I can pay quite well."

"Oh, no, no, thank you, sir, but no." He smiles, holding the door handle. "I can't carry a tune."

After he shuts the door behind him, I take a glass from the cabinet and fill it with three small bottles of whiskey. After the first gulp, the whiskey pushes painfully down my chest and spreads warmly through my body and out into my arms like scalding tea.

I walk over to the window and rest my forehead against the pane. In spite of the heat outside, the glass feels cool against a forehead filled with far too many destructive thoughts—a never-ending skein of thoughts that unrolls like the uninterrupted stream of news from countless TV channels where the difference between weather and ads is blurred beyond recognition. The direct broadcasts from war zones on various parts of the planet are the only reminders that day and night still have physical limits, and that somewhere, in faraway countries, it's still night.

Slowly, after several more glasses of whiskey, I calm down.

Outside, a blue darkness rests over a city in which there are twice as many cars as there are Danes in Denmark. In the ominously dark evening air, exhaust fumes shimmer like warm fog, making the lights of apartment complexes, high-rises, and mansions flicker and glow like smoldering bonfires. Up on the cliffs of Beverly Hills, the black, frayed palm groves recede, as though in anticipation of the light from the Great Quake that will ultimately burn down the city.

When you lose someone, you change—so the natural instinct is to preserve, to keep. In order to go on, you reach back, you brood. Maybe that's why I let myself go. Or maybe it's the booze.

One day, sometime in the future, we'll be sitting on a strange planet in the subdued light of a starship in Orion's outer belt, dreaming ourselves back to the forms and colors we once saw. Quick enough about getting away, we'll look at the last light of Earth in silent wistfulness and say to ourselves: How could we have? With keyboards and lightning-fast chips, we'll search through endless banks of data and pictures, and, like a laconic message from an unknown programmer's shaky hand, the answer will be in poetry: "The greatest beauty is beauty forever lost."

It's grown so dark behind the window that I can see my face in the glass before the light show inside begins. I topple clumsily to the floor. My knees hit the carpet and my face knocks against the windowpane with a hollow thud. Almost without a sound the whiskey spills across the carpet. A police helicopter flutters close to the hotel facade. This city! This country which taught its citizens to digest more pictures than the restless eye itself—and which reduces reality simply to picture and sound. It's like meeting the future.

In a few years they'll have five or six hundred TV channels. A cloud of photons will hover over the nation as digital lines connect New York to Los Angeles and the other large cities the way roads do today. I know this from my time in TV. I know the SECAM and NTSC systems by heart. I know why the French have a PAL system which, at least theoretically, makes their reception better than ours; and I know it's the number of lines on the screen that makes it impossible for us to exchange video tapes with the Americans but that also makes our reception better than theirs. I've forgotten the other details; we never really needed them.

The telephone rings. Louis.

"She leaves tomorrow. Her name is Natasha. Natasha Noiret."

Chapter Three

Behind tinted glass we glide along Route 405 as if we're on a ship, heading toward a dusty, desert-red sky. In a limousine with TV and free bar, the gin tastes like ether. But not even at the intersection near Inglewood and LAX does anyone outside press his nose against the glass. Around here movie stars and stretch limos are so common that a stranger on the street seems more exotic. One day, when I walked around Westwood, a middle-aged man—a total stranger—raised his hat in greeting.

I left behind the sweet, sickening smell of the orchids twining down the arch of the hotel entrance. I also left behind the hours I spent in front of my room's three TV screens. Even when I was brushing my teeth, I watched the news. The sleepy days were filled interchangeably with news and porno films; in the end it was hard to decide which channel was the most odious. I'd had enough. My friends Eva and Frank, who're also in the business, call it brilliantly analytical TV, but as far as I'm concerned, it could just as well be called hypothetical TV. I lived through forest fires, toxic spills, international crises—in the company of anchorpeople who moved like cartoon figures. Nothing actually *happened*. During the days of following images that moved by like one long comic book strip, we went through every conceivable variation of situations that never occurred. And I was filled with impotent depression: the one thing that the TV stations of the planet have made sure of is that we know immediately that there's nothing we can do.

What I wouldn't give right now to be sprawled on my own couch, or to be standing in the bay window watching beautiful women walk by.

The neighborhood's become so gentrified now, women sail along like unapproachable celebrities, the look in their eyes as steady as the gaze of cats, their movements as fluid as veil-tailed goldfish.

Monique was more beautiful than all of them. But now she's blue and pale and shrouded in darkness. I'll never again see her face in the twilight of the streetlamps, never again feel her small delicate breath, never again hear her chewing in her sleep as if she were eating cake in a dream café. And I'll never again nip at the soft little cushion under her chin, kiss her silky-dry lips, drowsily hear her whimper and feel her stir, then feel her sit bolt upright, until finally she loses patience and shakes me awake. Never again will I hear her say that she had that same stupid dream, looking hurt, as if I were the one who stuck it before her eyes. I'll never again feel her snuggle against me and make me promise that I'll never leave her, I'll never again feel the heat from her body and lie watching her until she wakes up, turns around, and pushes herself backward until we're lying together like spoons. Never again will I feel her hand reaching back and searching blindly down my arm until it finally settles, with a chubby little grip, around my finger. And never again will I look at the designs on her skin after a night's sleep—designs like secret symbols understood only by me. Her body's magic messages stamped into the folds of her skin. I'll never again read them on her back: all the words gone now, wiped away, forgotten, lost forever.

Her death woke me from a dream. When she died, something died in me. Maybe the dream itself. How would her death have affected me if it left me with visions of all the things we missed—all the things we never had time for, never could see together? Would I have been made poor in the loss or rich in the fantasy that would always remain unresolved in my head? If only I could somehow consummate my mourning. If only I had not learned more about her. As it is, now I must keep searching for more knowledge; I must know.

I recognize her right away; she's wearing the blue uniform again. When she stops in the middle of the hall, a halo of her hair is lit up by small white flames from a dusty sun burning its way through the cloud cover and the building's high glass dome. She walks up the stairs to the bar. I follow, then walk up behind her.

"I thought Danish flight attendants only lived at Doubletree Marina del Ray."

She turns.

"You again?" She smiles. "Normally we do."

"What will you have to drink?" I ask.

We sit down at one of the balcony tables in the departure hall. She's scanning the small sea of people below us.

"I'm waiting for a girlfriend." She looks at me with curiosity. "And what were *you* doing at the Four Seasons?"

"Working."

She smiles. "At the reception desk?"

If only her hair were lighter. She has the same features as Monique, same gestures, same full lips, same eyes. Still, there's something different, something that calls attention to itself, that always distinguishes the copy from the original. You can't put it into words. It's just there, like a feeling.

"Are you heading for Denmark, too?"

I nod. At that moment she spots her girlfriend in the stream of people below. She waves and signals that she's on her way, sips quickly at the glass on the table, then stops.

"Can I ask you a favor?" she asks. "I know it's terribly embarrassing, but would you mind carrying something through customs for me?"

"Now?"

"No, but I'll give it to you now. Unless you are going shopping."

I smile. "No, it's okay. What is it?"

She opens the bag. "Don't worry. It's not a bomb."

In the bag is a bottle, a carton of cigarettes, and a CD. That's all. I take the bag.

"It's so embarrassing to be caught with too much," she says. "Especially in my job. This is terribly sweet of you. I have to run now. I'll buy you a drink on the plane."

"They're free."

"Then perhaps you'll buy *me* one." She smiles, then gets up and hurries toward another woman in uniform down by the shops. When she reaches her, she turns around and smiles.

I realize that what I have to do is line up a row of stiff drinks in front of me on the plane. Before, I could handle the break—the mild depression—between pounding hangovers and the next drunk. Not anymore. In the hospital it was simple, I took a pill or a tablet. And they helped. Prozac, Valium, Melleril. I hardly know what I took; I just swallowed everything.

Dr. Phillip, the psychiatrist, was my doctor's idea. I'm in what they call outpatient treatment. They tell me it's good for me to talk about the dislocation of my psyche, the personal loss. They refuse to see that the incident, like a sprained ligament, will always be a weak point, it will never heal completely. Dr. Phillip doesn't see it either. And my skepticism irritates him.

"You seem rather . . . strong," he said during our first meeting. "Seem?"

I look down into the bag again. Then get up and walk out to the plane.

When I've found my seat in the cabin, I see her at the end of the long aisle in the front of the plane talking to her girlfriend. A little later they come toward me. While I'm stowing my hand luggage and jacket into the overhead compartment, I turn and see her three seats in front of me helping an elderly lady with her bags. She smiles at me, then goes back in the direction of the cockpit. I can see her legs through the slit of her skirt.

When the engines start up, I close my eyes; and when we move toward the runway, I think, as always, about death.

We fly in safe cabins as if they were space tunnels. We shoot through time and distance like mail through pneumatic tubes, stopping only to pass through gentle locks that function like cushions in the nexuses of the traffic network. But can fear itself destroy those safe metal networks? How many plane trips do I have left anyway? I mean, statistically?

I remember when I flew to Thailand to cover the coup. In the middle of the night, I woke up because the woman in the seat next to me was pulling at my arm. We were flying on the edge of a thunderstorm, and the jolts were quite powerful.

"I'm sorry," she said, "but I'm so scared of flying."

"It's quite all right."

"Do you mind?" She kept her hand on my arm.

Outside it was night. The cabin was completely quiet. Most people were asleep.

I looked at her. "It's okay," I said.

She looked deep into my eyes. "You were smiling in your sleep. What were you thinking about? Were you thinking about me?" she whispered. I felt her fingers caress my arm.

"I was thinking," I said in a low voice, "that I'd seen your stocking sag at the ankle, and now I'm sitting here thinking about the strip of bare white skin I can't see."

She crossed her legs. "Would you like to see it?"

The plane shook violently, and I could feel her nails through my shirt. Then the shaking returned to a faint, even rumble, and her grip loosened. She removed her hand and began discreetly unbuttoning her dress. After the last button, one side of her dress fell aside and I saw the edge of her stocking and a narrow white strip of thigh. She was sticky with moisture, and there was a shiny wet square on the inside of her thigh.

"Keep talking," she said.

With one hand between her legs, I spoke quietly to her and felt my cheeks flush. Several times I almost lost my voice while we rumbled along in the dark. She squirmed in her seat, her nails digging into my arm, and when we descended through a stairway of air pockets, she let out a series of gasps. She had enough presence of mind to time her screams so that they sounded like responses to the plane's jumps and lurches. Her other hand was in my crotch, rubbing efficiently until she felt the telltale jerks in her fingers and the small wet area of fabric. Other passengers farther forward in the plane were also gasping, and a few overhead compartment doors popped open, the jolts awakening one person after another.

The woman slid back and forth in her seat until she finally calmed down. She relaxed her grip on my arm; her nails had almost become embedded.

"I'm really sorry about that," she said.

"No problem."

"It really was quite innocent, wasn't it?" she said in the morning, when we parted.

"Not quite," I said. "You touched my arm." And I was thinking that I had become old before I was ever young, and I remembered that my friend Lindvig once said, "Innocence is something we lose when the people we desire squander it."

I doze in my seat, and wake with a start when we're ready for takeoff, Monique's picture imprinted on my retina—a picture that needs to be burned away with denial and strong drink.

Maybe the flight attendant is responsible for conjuring her up. Monique also flew for SAS.

A glimpse of the bare, synthetic inner thigh as she stumbles up the aisle. The uniform, the severity, the slit, and the bare thigh—this vulnerable nakedness hidden behind a thin, tight nylon veil.

I want to tear her open. Rip everything off her.

What's wrong with me? Am I a pervert? Did I catch some kind of Oriental fever? I feel like I'm wearing mittens, and postcoital melancholy is rushing through me.

Last year, Lindvig's cousin passed her university entrance exam.

"With that grade-point average, you can become anything you like," he said proudly.

"Can I?" she said. "How can I become happy?"

I stare at the food. A peculiar meal: flesh-colored crab salad in a little pastry basket, topped with a coin-sized slice of white lobster, and on top, like the pupil of an eye, a tiny piece of truffle: a terrified expression.

The gentleman next to me wants wine with his food.

"A bottle of Château, please," he says. He probably means Bordeaux or Bourgogne.

The flight attendant smiles thinly and quickly hands him a bottle of red wine.

Making nylon rubbing-together sounds, she carries the tray as securely as if it were a child hanging on to her. Warm, wet washcloths after the meal. The cloths stick together; with silver tongs she pokes and beats them as if they were strange limp fish being shaken out of a bird's beak.

Statistically speaking, there must be instances of lovemaking in the air. Perhaps at this very moment semen is running down her leg. And why did they pull the curtain a moment ago? Is the copilot getting a blow job? Was there time for a quickie in the customs-free zone? The cold click of buttons on uniforms; clothes unzipped like ripping skin.

But probably they're just preparing dinner.

When they start showing the movie, I get up and follow her.

It takes no more than a chrysalis of words and a hand on her arm. I'm not sure if it's the words or the light touch that does the trick, but soon we're chatting in the dusty light at the back of the cabin by the toilets. She laughs while her eyes search out my hands. Are my hands attractive? Is she imagining them on her skin? Or is she looking for something? A life line? A ring?

A couple of funny remarks, and a relentless flow of words that lovingly and excessively pay homage to her blue eyes that aren't that blue, her berrylike pout, her hands, her legs, the rippling of her breasts in the opening of the uniform, her big, blond, yarn-like hair, which—and this is only a thought—gives me a tickly feeling around the testicles, the fine, small, straight nose, the paper-white teeth, her smile, laugh, eyes. This flow of words made possible only because I took every free drink she offered.

This game. This dance which is so easy as long as you don't think about the steps.

There's no laughter inside this man, but she doesn't know that. There's no joy other than the kind he's offering right now. But she has no way of knowing that either. She can't possibly.

The invitation to her loins is eight-figured and written on a small scrap of paper. I crumple it up and put it in my pocket. There was another scrap of paper—the one I found among Monique's old things. "Jack Roth Pascal, Hotel Four Seasons, room 505." I was there. In my job, it's important to be there. It doesn't always pay off—you get used to that, but you've got to have been on the spot. A scrap of paper. We use paper in our world. Still use it. Lindvig says that it's only a question of time.

One of the flight attendants heads through the cabin past passengers who doze under blue blankets and the silent flow of images on the plane's video screen.

She wants to leave, but I stop her.

"Let me touch it," I say greedily, slipping a hand into her blouse.

"Not here," she says. But she doesn't tear herself away until I've massaged her nipple erect.

"What about the bag?"

"Now you've got my number," she says, smiling.

I quickly disappear into one of the toilets.

"Natasha? Where are you?" someone says.

From behind the door, the word sounds like an iron smoothing down cloth. Natasha. Natasha Noiret. Seductive alliterations that feel deliciously round in the mouth. Like Monique Milazar. A kind of rounding off, a way of enclosing the person, as though the person has something that needs to be concealed. A flaw.

I go back to my seat. When I finish skimming through the Danish newspapers, it's clear that the case is almost forgotten. Virtually no clues to Monique's murderer.

Chapter Four

At Kastrup Airport people open their umbrellas to escape the rain; frenetic tourists and business people hurry to find shelter in the doorways.

I collect my suitcases and walk out to the long line of wet, shiny vehicles. I put down my suitcases and look around for her. When I don't see her, I wait a while, then walk to the waiting taxis.

Still giddy from the long flight, I've abandoned a flight attendant I don't even know to foreign airports and new flight schedules. I've got a phone number and the lingering sensation in my fingers of a taut, rubbery nipple. It cost me my ration of duty-free cigarettes.

I hail a cab and go straight home. Green, windblown, dotted with small houses, the island of Amager glides past the car window. Sheets of rain stream down the windshield, pushed away by the large wiper.

"Vacation?" the driver asks.

"Work. Hard work."

I slide back into the seat. The motor is almost silent, hardly more than a whisper. The smoothness of the automatic gear shift numbs like a tranquilizer.

It's pouring.

At Monique's funeral the rain was as fine as dust. Four weeks ago now, it feels like years. Or like seconds.

That day, the drizzle was imperceptible, almost tender, like tiny grains of damp, multicolored powder falling on the crowd of black-clad people who walked, heads bowed, gravel crunching under their feet on the cemetery path. Everyone walked slowly, stiffly, as if simply by delaying they could hold back what had already happened.

I walked close to her parents but was totally removed from their pain, which had transformed them into contorted, almost unrecognizable strangers. Her mother's beautiful face was collapsed into itself, as if the muscles and cheekbones had been removed; its parting gift to Monique was to surrender its beauty. Her father's face was thin and ashen, his eyes swollen and red.

One tries to let go of the pain. One tries so hard to imagine what happened. How final this ritual was. But it seems easier for the elderly, who live closer to death and who have been through this before.

The faces of the relatives and distant, almost forgotten acquaintances who walked by with small, peculiar grimaces and handshakes that were never allowed time to grip properly. They stepped aside quickly to make room for others on line, as though they expected to be reproached or slapped, or as though they felt impotent, that they'd lost the words that no one could find.

Standing a bit off to the side as the coffin was lowered into the ground, Inspector Klinker kept a respectful distance throughout the ceremony. He kept running his hand through his limp, thinning hair. He didn't come over.

Eva and Frank were wonderful. So was Lindvig. I leaned on them for support. Lindvig even gave me a dry kiss on the cheek.

Afterward, on our way to an inn for coffee, I was walking in front of Eva and Frank. I know that they didn't know I heard them, and I also know that it wasn't meant maliciously.

Eva whispered, "Did you see the newspaper?"

"Yours or mine?"

"Mine."

"That's no paper . . ."

The world is so confused and hurried, as though there's always something we have to get past, as though we're trying to bring to a conclusion something we never finished in order to have time for something we never started.

The taxi crosses the bridges to the city. In the gray fog and rain, Copenhagen is all roofs and spires. The only thing that seems alive is the shiny black asphalt: expressionistic paintings in reflections from the red, yellow, and green traffic lights. It's still only afternoon, but a heavy cloud cover makes it seem already dark.

The driver checks his rearview mirror. I turn to look. A black Mazda is right behind us.

"Is he tailing us?"

"In traffic there's always someone behind you," the driver says.

We stop at an intersection. Traffic lights, girls jaywalking through the red light. Using its brights, another car signals us out into an opening in the traffic; only one of the lights is working, it is like a wounded, metallic animal, one eye hanging in shreds. We ease forward.

Just before we reach my street, I turn to look again. The black Mazda is gone.

The taxi driver gets out to open the door and helps me with my bags. The young woman in the building opposite mine stands at the window.

"It turned at the intersection," the driver says.

I smile and take out my money. "Which way?"

"Left," he says. "No. Yes, he went left."

"Then it's them. They've been after me a long time."

I pay and walk to the door. When I look up again at her window across the street, she's gone. In the alley between the buildings the sun is trying to break through the thick clouds. I unlock the door and struggle up the stairs with my suitcases. As I reach the door, I hear the phone ring. With the pile of mail, advertisements, and old newspapers on the floor inside, I have to shove the door hard to get in.

I reach the phone before the answering machine kicks in. Dr. Phillip.

"Mr. Molberg, I just wanted to remind you about tomorrow."

"I'll be there."

"It's important that we talk."

"So you say."

"What do you mean by that, Mr. Molberg?"

"What exactly do you want?"

"To help."

"Help whom?"

He's silent for a moment, then says, "Did you remember to take your pills?"

"I remember everything."

Inside it's complete chaos.

On the wall in the hallway under the two full-length, gold-leaf-framed mirrors, the gilded consoles have been pulled out of their hinges. The living room is littered with bottles and broken glass; the light from outside reflects in the green and crimson glass like strange, unpolished stones. The wine-red chaise lounge stands in the center of the room like a furry, velvet island. The pictures are askew except for the one in the gold-leaf frame. Vases are knocked over. Two chairs are locked into each other as in an embrace, or as if they're keeping each other from falling. Above the window the handle of the venetian blinds has been pulled down and bent to one side. The bay window has a jagged streak down the glass, as though struck by some large, blunt object: the shards of a drama, like feathers and streaks of blood in the snow. On the floor are letters I never should have read but which I read again and again, looking for a solution, a secret code that, if broken, could have led to a deeper truth. All I found was a crumpled note with the name Jack Roth Pascal and the name of a hotel in Los Angeles.

It looks as if they have searched all three rooms and the bedroom facing the street, even the kitchen on the other side of the apartment. They have searched and found nothing. In the rumbling blue darkness I walk to the massive, cast-iron, coarse-tiled cooking island. The cabinets are open, pots and pans scattered all over the tiles. Not even my workroom facing the courtyard has been spared. This is where I keep my past—what's left of it. Pictures and books that were on the shelves are now scattered all around. My trophies lie tossed like so many dishes on the floor.

In the middle of the mess I spot the tear-gas capsule. Though it has a small dent on one side, it's still intact. I bought it for Monique once when I was in France and smuggled it through customs. But she never carried it. If she'd had it with her that night, it might have saved her. I've seen those capsules spurt. They work.

Outside it's dusk. The last golden, almost sacred light fades from the bay window. I walk through the piles of glass and junk.

A light comes on in the apartment of the young woman across the street. She's behind her curtain like a shadow, but I don't know if she sees me. Then she draws her curtains, and the light goes out. In the apartment directly across from me the lights, as always, are off. Zenia on the top floor insists it's rented, but I think it's empty. There's never any light.

Right after the funeral I went into the hospital. The apartment looked just like it does now—a big mess. I lay on the floor for several days, like a discarded rug. All I did was drink. Got no sleep. Just lay there, sodden and heavy, as if I'd lost a lot of blood. Weakness filled my body like a falling wave.

Finally I called for a doctor to give me something to help me sleep. When he finally came, I'd fallen asleep. I remember thinking how funny it was that he had to wake me up to give me something to put me to sleep.

He asked a few questions. I talked a lot about stress on the job and made up some heavy financial problems. I also touched on the argument with Monique. On the prescription he wrote, "For heartbreak." Cute. When it happened again a few days later, I was admitted.

To think that I mentioned the argument but didn't mention that she was dead. I wasn't myself. That's my only excuse: I wasn't myself. At the newspaper I told them I was sick, and to my friends I said I needed time alone.

I place my finger on the windowpane and for a moment let it rest in the scratch. What really happened here? Did I mix everything up into one big cocktail? And was that when the window-pane was scratched? Was I trying to get out? I don't remember. There are some things we just don't remember—usually fairly insignificant things, but sometimes the most important.

In the half-light the answering machine blinks red from its place in the bookcase. I crunch my way over to it, rewind, and listen as I start to clean up. There's a message from Mimi; she left the number of the bank. When I got back from the hospital, I used to be filled with anticipation coming home to the blinking answering machine. It was as if some unknown voice would change my life. Maybe that was because of the call I did get.

I take the container of pills out of my bag and put it on the bathroom shelf, then change my mind. I take off the cover and sprinkle a few into the toilet bowl, then pour out a few more before I replace the cover: they disappear in a cloud of fizz. I hide the container at the back of the medicine cabinet.

When I call Klinker, his wife answers.

"Just a moment," she says. "Max, it's for you."

He comes to the phone.

"Molberg, where are you?"

"Home."

"Where have you been?"

"I took a trip. I hope that's not against the law."

"No, no. What do you want?"'

"Someone broke into my place."

"I see. What did they take?"

"Nothing." I walk over to the bay window and stare out. She's not there. At least I can't see her.

"Doesn't it seem curious to you?" I say.

He's breathing heavily.

"Molberg, you're still seeing your doctor, aren't you?"

I hang up.

While I struggle with the venetian blind handle, I see her. The old lady across the way. Her eyes are accusing me of something. Or is she just lost in thought, looking out the window aimlessly?

I don't see her very often; it's only recently that I've begun to notice her. I'm not the type to spy on people, though I have to admit that I often peek over at the young woman, who almost never closes her curtains. But that's another story; after all that's happened, she interests me.

Maybe that's what the old lady is reproaching me for; she thinks I'm a Peeping Tom. I pan from the young woman back past the empty apartment to the old lady.

Suddenly a shudder runs through her body. Something looks wrong, out of place. Maybe she reads the wrong newspapers, or maybe she's ill. Or maybe some small thing that was gnawing at her has suddenly been blown out of proportion.

She's hunched over. Her whole body is shaking.

I think: something, anything, can hit us out of the blue so suddenly that it looks as if we're succumbing to a long-guarded sorrow. Have I always carried around an image inside me? Has she? Do we all carry hidden images inside? We're so vulnerable when something touches feelings that long ago lost any connection to the particular images that distorted them, images that carry us forward. Unconsciously. Toward a blinding white light that melts us. Like insects.

The telephone rings.

"It's me."

For a moment I'm not sure. But slowly the words define her. The flight attendant from the flight. She must have looked up my number.

"How's Friday?"

"Friday's fine," I say.

Maybe it's the exhaustion of the trip. Or the little melody in her voice which for a brief moment makes it sound as if this is a voice that can change my life.

There was that other call. Whenever we talk, Dr. Phillip fishes for it. But I don't know what to tell him. Besides, I don't want to. When the telephone rang that evening, I'd already decided to go. One shouldn't make too much of calls like that. I've had several from people who grunted, laughed, or promised to beat the shit out of me. What made that particular call interesting wasn't what was said but what wasn't. There was just silence on the other end. The interesting thing was the click on the line. It was a call from another country.

Chapter Five

"We've tried you several times."

"I've been away."

"Well, that explains it," he says, looking around the large, bright room filled with customers and bank employees. "I think we'll go to my office."

I follow him behind the counter.

"Right this way."

We walk among desks of bank people working away at their keyboards and telephones. They look up and smile politely as we pass.

"Please, sit down," he says, shutting the door. "Can I offer you something? Coffee?"

"Yes, please."

"Just a moment." He disappears down the hallway, leaving the door open.

I look around his sparsely furnished office. Instead of what would be a white stained beech or oak table in many yuppie offices, there is an old, heavy teak desk; on it is nothing but a push-button phone and a small tabletop drawer arrangement. A ballpoint pen lies on the papers he's brought along. I stretch in my chair and try to read upside down, but I still can't figure out what he wants. I lean back in my chair and study the two prints on the wall above his chair. I wonder if anyone before me has ever even noticed them. Maybe waiting customers, but who else? It's always been a mystery to me why modern art is hung in places where the clientele isn't the least bit receptive to the challenges of abstract forms. Think of what the bank is selling and the customers consuming: deficits, annuities, saving accounts, mortgages, pension installments. All prose, no poetry. Financial arabesques whose forms are the squares and frames of cubism and whose content is wholly literal. At the obligatory receptions and banquets that bank executives attend, maybe they've picked up a vocabulary for describing the abstract, so that, at least on an intellectual level, they can comment on the Deeper Meaning of the work. But to the bank employees, these pictures must be closed mysteries, things invisible to them. To themselves and the customers, their disciples, bank employees preach a religion of tight forms and tight budgets, while at home they renounce their own words, deny their own God: everyone knows that bank employees are poorly paid and the most irresponsible consumers.

I don't know him; Monique was in charge of dealing with the bank. Vice President Stuhr—the branch manager—enters with the coffee and clears his throat.

"We read about it. Terrible! And she was so young. Well, I'm sure you know what we called you about."

I smile accommodatingly. I have no idea what it's all about, but after the offer of coffee I reject the possibility that I unwittingly did something illegal——a thought that I'd actually been entertaining since the bank called me. People who write phony checks are not offered coffee, and besides, from the moment I set my foot in the door, the atmosphere has been embracing, warm, cordial, as though we have something in common. Only I don't know what it is, aside from the fact that it must have something to do with money.

"I'm not absolutely sure," I say, careful not to say too much or too little.

"The account," he says.

"The account?"

"Your, how should I say, joint account. Of course you know about it?"

"Of course."

He's young, much younger than you'd expect a bank manager to be. He looks up with his banker's look, half resigned, half reproachful, as if we really ought to have discussed this thoroughly at home. And then his everything-for-the-customer smile, which, in spite of his inner loathing, tells me that the bank exists for people like me.

It finally dawns on me that we're sitting in the bank's inner sanctum. Ordinary customers, even rather well-to-do ones, are usually attended to outside, at the counter, or by one of the middle-level employees at their desks in the arena. Only customers with a lot of money, or VIPs——which pretty much amounts to the same thing——are invited into the manager's private office. Since neither of these categories fits me, I'm still not clear what he's going to tell me. I pull out a cigarette.

He pushes himself backward a bit and searches through his desk drawers, then places an ashtray on the table. Finally he says:

"At some point your fiancée mentioned the possibility of placing the money in securities, the bank's own securities, that is."

I smile indulgently. That's about the only possibility left: Monique left behind yet another secret. One more thing she did not tell me. Just like the photograph. And the scrap of paper with the name Jack Roth Pascal. I rummage around in my pocket for a Thorazine. I don't know what to say, but I feel an automatic hostility toward him because he knows something I don't—something I want to know.

"I don't think she could have been serious," I say.

"Well, of course, that's entirely up to you now."

Suddenly I'm overcome with disgust—for him, for myself, and for Monique, whose secrets put me in all these awkward situations. I'm wondering if, at this very moment, Vice President Stuhr is gloating inwardly. Has he seen through me? Is he sitting there feeling sorry for me? Oh, you didn't know? Your fiancée, your intimate companion, kept a secret from you. An account. An amount. But who knows, maybe there's nothing strange about it at all.

How big is *his* salary? Or is this his way of getting his jollies? His head is bent over his papers, and I stare furiously at his high forehead and his hair, which frizzes away from his head with a burnt look just like Inspector Klinker's. I'm seized with a great desire to pick up something heavy and smash in his skull. The disgust. The inescapable misery of being constantly placed in situations where you have to talk to people you wouldn't ordinarily have anything to do with. Despicable people. For a moment I wonder if Mr. Nicholson would have accepted the stock offer. But of course he's got people who handle this sort of thing. Or he'd simply buy the bank.

So this is the reason for the meeting. At the time of her death Monique Milazar left an unspecified but not insignificant sum of money in the bank. Not in her own account but in a joint account. A joint account. It wouldn't have been like Monique to invest her money in securities, so either she was trying to please him by considering the possibility of buying some bank stock, or the enterprising manager sees the opportunity of unloading some of the stock onto an unsuspecting surviving partner: why else would he stick his nose in our business? If the second theory is true, then he's a purely cynical, calculating man trying to take advantage of a naive and therefore undoubtedly kind-hearted person who wouldn't dream of going against the last wishes of the deceased.

"How much was she thinking of?" I say.

"Half."

I look at his eyes staring hard at me. I wonder if it's mean-spirited neighbors or people like him who make anonymous calls to the tax department. I finally realize that we're bargaining.

"Some rather substantial amounts were deposited," he says.

"When?"

"In March of this year."

"Did you speak to the police about it?"

"No, there's no reason to . . . now."

I've been trying to pretend that I know about the account, and I'm sure he knows I don't know. Of course I knew it existed. Monique and I opened it for vacations. But I don't know the amount. I'd like to. And he'd like to get his hands on it.

"I'll think it over," I say. "I may consider a third. In that case, how much would be left?"

"Well, there would still be a substantial amount."

I lean over the desk and crush out my cigarette.

"Exactly how much?"

"At the moment the money is in an ordinary savings account, so the interest isn't very high. But that's the way she wanted it. That's why we were considering the possibility of . . ."

"How much?"

"Two million crowns."

I have no idea what to say. It's as though I'd prepared myself to think that the scope of Monique's crime was directly proportional to the size of the amount. And that, in turn, the dimensions of my suffering would be a direct extension of that amount. In the course of the conversation, it began to dawn on me that we weren't talking about a small sum, but I hadn't imagined anything like this. A couple of hundred thousand. Maybe a quarter of a million, but nothing like this.

The manager is watching me.

"Does the amount surprise you?"

Finally I pull myself together. I shake my head. "Listen. I'll leave a million in the account, and the rest you can invest in stock."

He brightens.

"That is, aside from the half million I need right now."

I get up and shake his hand.

"There'll be some papers for you to sign," he says nervously.

"You can just send them to me. I trust you implicitly. And I promise to buy your stock."

"Very well, very well," he says, a bit perplexed. "Let's go out to the teller."

They hand me the money in large bills. There's a certain excitement in the air, even from the woman counting the stacks of bills.

Afterward, Vice President Stuhr walks me all the way to the

door. The woman is left with the illusion that she's just dealt with one of the lucky ones. Someone with money. Can they check me out on their computers? Pry into Monique Milazar's hidden kingdom? Perhaps they have dreams of instant transformation too. But it will never happen; they're too sensible to gamble. In their tight budgets there's no room for games and the lottery, so unless they inherit money or commit a crime, they'll be right here after many perfunctory raises and twenty years of faithful service. Nothing will ever change. Every day they'll sit with huge sums, incredible wealth within their grasp, but it'll be the customers' money no matter what stocks or bonds they invest in. Every day for years they'll sit here with their frustrations and self-torment, their envy and small burning hatred for those who *have*. And there'll be no way to get rid of that anger, except perhaps by offering low interest rates to customers deep in debt. But when the customers then move to a friendlier bank, the employees will be the ones to get blamed. It's never good to lose customers.

The truth is that wealth is no blessing. Wealth is penury. Two million crowns have made me poorer.

"I promise you won't regret it," says the young manager, holding the door for me.

"How do you know what I'll regret?"

Then I leave. No one stops me.

We had two years together, Monique and I. And I'm beginning to see that I never knew her.

I drive to work to pick up my newspapers and old mail. Neither Solker nor Borris is there. Then I drive around the harbor past the freight terminals and out to Fredriksholms Inlet and the North Pier, looking at the ships heading up through the Strait of

Øresund. A faint westerly wind is blowing, but it's balmy. Beyond the ships are white dots of seagulls and the majestic honking of ferries. I smoke a cigarette, then take out the picture and stare at it. Her contorted face. His eyes dripping with sweat. I have to find a way to deal with this. I can't understand how people can take pictures like that. I never photographed Monique naked; I don't even have a picture of her without a bra. I cannot associate her with that picture.

I knew a man who worked in one of the large photography chains. He told me that once a week he and a few colleagues got together to look through people's private photos—the most intimate ones, of course. That tradition's probably over now that so many people use the one-hour services.

"You can't imagine what people take pictures of," he said and promised me that one evening I could join them. But it never happened.

I study the picture. Can't take it in. I try to distance myself from her, to see her as a stranger. It's the only way I can deal with it.

Afterward I just make it to my own bank before it closes. It pleases me that they take the bundles of money without a fuss; I was worried that they might ask all sorts of questions. I look around, but no police come rushing in to arrest me. Nothing at all happens.

"Lotto?" asks the woman behind the counter.

"No, actually that's not it."

"So many people are winning these days." Flirtatiously she places the receipt on the counter for my signature.

"By the way, my divorce just came through," she says with a smile.

"In a way, so did mine."

The drive out of town, past the fields, past the lakes.

Beeches with buds ready to burst. Cool white and pink foliage line the small residential streets. May. On my way along the familiar old roads, memories meet me halfway.

Monique in May sun. How she sat laughing and talking one wet summer which I remember as full of sun. Evenings as darkness fell when I watched her small hands holding a mug of tea. Twilight hours behind a row of spruce trees with a strange coolness between our legs.

"Act like grownups!" we were told when she—as she often did—walked on my feet with her arms around my neck.

Since then we've hardly spoken of her. And I've hardly seen them.

When I arrive, Mother's in the garden. She stands in her boots by the flower bed near the road. She doesn't know I'm here; her gloved hands pinch at the ground close to the hedge until, with a sigh, she straightens and sees me walking up the garden path. She bangs her hoe on the ground to knock the dirt off and throws the weeds into the wheelbarrow.

"Are you staying for dinner?" she asks.

"Not if it's too much trouble."

"I just need to know if I should take something out." She pulls off her gloves. "We don't see you very often."

I give her a little hug. "The doctor says it's important."

"To avoid us?"

"To see you."

It's late in the afternoon. The sun is pouring through the tall, undulating birches in the backyard.

"Do you want coffee?" she asks, and we go inside.

I sit down on a kitchen chair while she puts a filter in the cone and pours in the coffee.

"Why aren't you at work?"

"I have a couple of days off. But I wrote something on my last trip. Haven't you seen the paper?"

"You know Dad reads the other one. Was it London?"

"America. I met Jack Nicholson."

"Oh," she says. "What about John Wayne?"

"Mom, he's dead."

"Oh, yes. By the way, your brother got the job in Singapore. He called the other day. Kirsten and the baby are going, too."

There must have been happy days. Long days without yearning, days full of carefree smiles, kisses that we drank like dew, movements unhindered by self-consciousness. Now it's as if others, ghostly creatures wearing our faces, make our moves for us. Monique's death has come between us. That, and a lot of other things. The pile is growing.

Dr. Phillip says that we all carry around some baggage inside. "Odd that so many of us consider our childhood our happiest time," he says. But isn't that perhaps because it was? Perhaps childhood was actually so happy that ever since, our expectations have fallen short.

After dinner, Dad collapses on the couch.

"Did you see the paper?" I ask.

"Nah."

"I interviewed Jack Nicholson."

He doesn't react.

"He may be buying a bank soon," I say.

"Nikkelsen? Is he the one with the Westerns?"

"Nicholson. No, that's John Wayne."

"Wayne. He died a while ago."

"Yes. I was over there for a while."

"Did you hear your brother's being sent abroad?"

Maybe it's just too unreal for them. Monique and I lived another life. In a few years I've seen more of the world than they have in their whole lives. I've lived in hotels they can only fantasize about, and I've been on the front lines of a war they think they know only because they watched it on TV. They're hard to talk to. Somehow there seems to be nothing to talk about. We are watching a Cary Grant movie, but Mom is nodding off and Dad is snoring on the couch. They've grown old. I don't know what the change is really about. When we sit this way in the screen's blue light, it's as if this is how it's always been. But when I walk down the garden path and Mom stands waving in the doorway, I always feel like going back and saying something. But I don't know what.

There was a time when I thirsted for their love. Their recognition. Now I don't know. Maybe I still want it. But I'm no longer sure why. Maybe so that I can reject it.

Chapter Six

He opens the door himself. As we walk down the hallway, a woman, presumably his wife, flutters like a quick shadow across the living-room wall.

Dr. Phillip asks about my trip. I tell him that everything went well: I collapsed a few times, but I also did some good work.

He smiles. But doesn't like my collapsing that way.

"Did you remember the pills?"

"Yes," I say.

He still doesn't have a clear overview, he says. He'd like a more precise picture of my suffering. I try my best, but can't. He looks at me, pondering.

"In other words, it was pretty much everything?"

"Yes."

"Well, that's quite common."

Now that we've established the parameters of my suffering, he seems satisfied—even if the parameters have been extended to include everything.

There he sits behind his desk. Dr. Phillip. With his dark hair, glasses, and commanding gaze. Arms folded, an elbow resting in one hand, his lips in a pout. Slowly, very slowly, he brings his forefinger to his pursed lips.

He's trying to cajole and worm his way toward a "usable" breakdown—something more than just uncontrollable rage. But he's warned me that the therapy might become rather unpleasant at times. Maybe one day I really will break down.

"Terrible things may emerge," he says. "Some of my . . . uh, clients fall apart. They weep and say the most shocking things."

He says this with a worried expression, but it seems to me that he's almost hopeful. As he taps his pouting lips with his finger, he looks at me thoughtfully, then says that he'd like to return to that night, the one during the week after the funeral.

"What exactly happened?"

"I started feeling bad," I say.

"Why do you think you started feeling bad?"

"Why not?"

"What exactly were you doing? Watching TV? Rummaging through old things?"

"I was packing up some of Monique's stuff."

"And then it just started?"

"Yes."

"Did something specific make you think of her?"

"I'd just lost her."

"There wasn't any particular thing, something you found?"

"What are you getting at?"

With a slightly annoyed expression Dr. Phillip says that I have to learn to let go. Not be so suspicious. He says that I think too much. Intellectualize. Pronounced obsessive-compulsive behavior, he says. It may have no connection to all the other issues, but of course that's what we're trying to determine.

"Try to say what you're feeling."

"That's what I'm doing. I don't feel anything at all."

"Not even when you think of that evening?"

"Nothing."

Dr. Phillip leans back in his chair. Behind him the bookcase is full of weighty books. Tall, small, thick, thin, pamphlets, booklets, case histories, reference books, encyclopedias. The whole artillery of heavy thoughts.

"I regard illness as a prerequisite for health, but of course you always have to contend with people's prejudices."

He has his own troubles, he's confided to me. That was when he was trying to win me over with the preliminary tactics of intimacy. "Without trust we might as well hang it up" is what he said.

At times he looks as though he almost relishes the thought. Perhaps there's a heroic martyr in him, a man of overweening ambition. Maybe he dreams of changing the world the way his famous mentor did. But he gets irritated when the analysand thinks he's detected projection on the part of the analyst. It's not my job to analyze, he says. I'm only disrupting the therapy.

"I assume you're aware that exaggerated intellectualizing at the expense of feeling is actually quite pathological?" he says.

I smile at the sight of Dr. Phillip tapping his lips in front of all those bookcases groaning under the weight of endless rows of books.

I know I think too much, and I know that he believes that we're dealing with an obsessive-compulsive neurosis. But it seems like we're dealing with a lot of things. The diagnosis seems to change all the time.

"A lot of wreckage may turn up," he says, "even if the starting point was quite a different one."

Like cars. You bring them to the mechanic and get them back

with new problems. Or hospitals: if you're not already sick, you will be.

Dr. Phillip leafs through his papers. "What about that call you got?"

I look at him uncomprehendingly. "I don't remember . . ."

He bends over his papers. "It says here that you mentioned something about a call."

"When was that?"

"You told me about it the day you got out of the hospital."

"I mean, when was I supposed to have got the call?"

He checks his papers. He knows nothing.

"It doesn't say."

I shake my head. "Doesn't ring a bell."

He looks at me skeptically. Then gives up.

It will all come back to you, he insists with an almost messianic expression. It will come to you through our talks. But he's always changing his diagnosis. At first I was supposed to be suffering from severe manic-depression. Something that had happened long before Monique. Its sudden reoccurrence was triggered by losing her.

"Obviously it's reactive. Obviously."

But perhaps it's endogenous. You never know. You can never be sure.

"In that case it'll undoubtedly take time, and be harder to access."

It keeps changing. One moment I'm merely neurotic; the next, almost schizophrenic. When I try to play it all down, Dr. Phillip asks me pedagogically if I know what a neurosis really is. I say that it sounds like some kind of fishing tackle. He returns to where he started.

"We've just got to prune the worst off the top," he says.

"Oh, just a little hedge-trimming?"

He's tapping his lips again.

"You could call it that."

"You would have made a fine gardener, Doctor."

Dr. Phillip's problem is that there are so many possibilities. Thousands. And most likely none of them is right. That's probably why we've chosen to believe in a few of them, and then created little gods out of the people who thought them up.

But even though I have reservations about everything Dr. Phillip says and thinks, of course he's right. Every day I walk around in a swarm of thoughts. Thoughts of absolutely everything. Why I do what I do and not something else. Why I am what I am and not someone else. What kind of illness I'm dragging around and exactly how I got it.

I can understand the dislocation of my psyche, the one I drown every night in alcohol, but in spite of the infantile repetition of certain thoughts over and over again, as Dr. Phillip calls these incessant, repeated excursions along the same patterns of ideas, it's still hard for me to think of myself as ill.

"But I function," I say.

"It may be difficult for you to understand this," Dr. Phillip says, "but that's exactly what's sick."

"That I function?"

"That you function so well."

Dr. Phillip is also unhappy about our agreement to discuss the diagnosis, but I insist. Ignoring his protests and watching him squirm, I threaten not to show up for the appointments and the weekly pill handouts.

He thinks I'm living in a false euphoria.

"You're like a man with diabetes," he says. "Without the pills you become someone else."

"Oh, now you're scaring me."

He looks at me, irritated. "It's not funny."

"No. One can die of fright."

Of course he's familiar with my hospital and police reports, but he doesn't place much credence in them. There's been so much irregularity, as he calls it, and raises his hand as if to stop me before I start.

"Everyone makes mistakes. Don't take it personally. Did it feel good to get away?"

I shrug.

"All right," he says. That's his way of saying that now we should get started. "It's important, vital, that at this point we work everything through."

"And why is that?"

"Because if we don't, it'll hit you much harder the next time."

I look at him.

"There won't be a next time."

Chapter Seven

A liquid the consistency of clear shampoo runs down her face. Like thick tears, or sperm. She flicks her tongue out of the corner of her mouth and tastes. Then rubs it into her cheeks and down her throat.

"They say it's good for the complexion," she says.

She didn't even have time to take her clothes off. She'd changed into her own clothes in the back of the taxi on the way from the airport. When I looked amazed, she laughed and told me that the driver was a woman. Her suitcases in the hallway are in a jumbled heap.

Natasha Noiret. Such a musical name. Like a mantra. Like whispering evenings or velvety sleep.

She tells me that her name was supposed to have been Rikke or Lone, but her father thought that they sounded like dogs' names.

Her eyes. Do I detect a certain reserve? Monique's eyes let all the light in.

While I go to the kitchen to open bottles, she explores the apartment.

"Who's this?" she says. She's holding up a picture of Monique.

"It's over now."

"What does she do?"

"The same as you."

"You mean, she's up to no good?"

The dining table by the bay window glows with fresh fruit and, direct from her trip to Paris, foie gras topped with chopped bullion jelly, like sticky gold. The fizz of champagne pricks our faces as we toast each other. The champagne glasses belonged to Monique. As I look around, I realize that almost everything here belonged to Monique. It's not something you think about. You just keep going.

Glancing over at the woman in the apartment across the street, I see that as usual she hasn't drawn her curtains. Maybe she doesn't realize how much you can see from here. Maybe she's sitting in the dark; at night she almost always sits in the dark. The only light I see is from her TV screen. I often think that she should put on some lights. To protect her eyes.

With a lascivious smile, Natasha pushes herself away from the table, spreading her legs slightly. She hitches up her skirt a little.

"What do you want for dessert?"

Then she pulls her skirt all the way up and puts one foot on the edge of the table, caressing the lacy pattern of her panties. Underneath, her sex is a dark shadow.

I tell her to go put on her uniform.

She squints. Then smiles.

Flipping her legs off the table, she gets up and smoothes down her skirt. Obediently she walks into the hallway, picks up her suitcase, and goes into the bedroom to change.

Once upon a time I dreamed like a young girl. Of drinking toasts under pale moons by roaring oceans. Of stepping into the wet, sandy footprints of people who'd walked there before us.

But fantasies of that kind of magical love quickly vanished. The first time I got drunk, and felt the surprise rush of alcohol in my bloodstream, I was pawing a girl a few years older than me. My hands seemed to lose all connection to me. Before she knew it, she was laid. It was so easy. Nothing to it. Just a move a fraction of a second faster than her protest. That was before Monique.

As she stands there in her uniform, I wonder if perhaps she met Monique. Maybe they flew together, or accidentally bumped into each other in a ladies' room somewhere on the other side of the planet.

The scar down my left cheek is like ragged stitching on a scrap of fabric. It's sexy, says Natasha. She shuts her eyes and lets her finger trace it like a blind person trying to read a message in the seam. I got it when I was little; a friend accidentally hit me with a spade. When anyone asks, I say a dog bit me.

I tell her to lie on the bed. She walks to the headboard and holds it while she wriggles out of her shoes. Then she unbuttons the uniform slightly and steps out of her panties, which land on the floor like a small, crumpled napkin.

There she lies, eyes shut, scratching the sheets like a cat being stroked.

I get two silk ties from the closet and tie her hands to the headboard.

But when I want to blindfold her, she protests.

"I don't want that. I don't like it," she says.

"Yes, you do," I say. "You just don't know it."

She sleeps heavily. Her cheeks are bruised red from the stubble on my chin. Or from the release of a lust so powerful it burns through her skin.

I get up and start cleaning up the worst of the mess. While I'm carrying bottles and ashtrays into the kitchen, she suddenly appears in the doorway, dark and dangerous, wrapped in a sweater that she's somehow managed to make look like a form-fitting little party dress. She pulls it down tightly so that her nipples stand out, brown and bumpy, but I have to chase her around tables and chairs to catch her.

Snorting, I land of top of her. I hold down her hands, pull off her sweater, and push a hand between her legs. Her naked crotch is dripping. I kiss her all the way down her belly and bury my face between her legs. Then I rub my face around in her sex, nipping and sucking at the delicate, rosy colors. Her Venus mound is exposed and tender, like a tulip ready to burst open.

She sighs. I lie on top of her.

"Playing hard to get?"

"Carnivores have to be allowed to play with their prey before they eat it," she says.

I kiss the groove of her neck and push one joint of a finger inside her.

"You're a lovely prey," I say.

She tilts her head backward, exposing her throat.

"Who says *I'm* the prey?" She says.

Chapter Eight

"Oh, I love it."

"The juice?"

"No, the sperm. It's running out of me."

We're sitting at the breakfast table. She's only wearing panties. And the T-shirt she borrowed from my closet. Her breasts stand out through the fabric like shadows.

"Don't you have any pictures of Monique?" she asks while we drink coffee.

"Why?"

"It's nice to know what I'm up against. You don't talk about her much. What did she do to you?"

"I thought women hated to hear about old flames."

"There are exceptions," she says.

"Such as?"

"When they're *that* beautiful," she says and points to the stack of photographs.

She picks up one of them, studying it carefully. "It makes you curious."

"About what?"

She looks at me. "About finding out what went wrong."

"It's over now," I say.

"What's over?"

I don't know why I don't tell her anything. It just seems wrong. It also seems wrong to show her the pictures. It's as if Monique is still floating through the rooms, invisible, inviolable, silent, fluttering the curtains when she needs fresh air. I also don't understand why Natasha hasn't heard about it. Read about it. I can't make her out.

I show Natasha the other pictures. Vacation pictures, party pictures, beach pictures, birthdays, Christmas. Also from my work, from Parliament (showing The Reporter in his very young days), and from the coup in Thailand. Natasha asks for names, dates, events, but is particularly curious about Monique's work pictures.

"Strange that I never saw her," she says.

"Are you sure you never saw her?"

She squints. "Do you think I'm lying?"

I smile and start collecting the photos. "Of course not."

"Is that all you have?" she says, looking over the table.

"Isn't it enough?"

"It's never enough."

She helps me gather the pictures, which I put into the box with the others. She looks at her watch, then gets up. "I have to get going."

As in a haze I see her image as she stands by the bay window phoning for a taxi. She asks about the scratch in the window-pane; I tell her it's always been there. And suddenly it strikes me that the police may simply have missed it the night they were here. Maybe it's been there all the time. Ever since she died. But I push away the thought. I know that's not what happened.

While she puts on her coat, she looks thoughtful. Then she grabs my collar and kisses me. She pulls away a bit and looks at me.

"This wasn't what I intended at all," she says.

"What wasn't?"

"All this kissing."

"It sounds as if you'd planned the whole thing."

She smiles. "Maybe."

Maybe it's the uniform that does it. And how much she looks like Monique.

At the door, she turns to me. "Wednesday? Dinner? The Three Towers?"

I nod.

She kisses my cheek, then turns my face and rubs away the lipstick. Monique did that, too.

"The bag," she says.

I get it for her, open it, and look inside. "It's all there."

And then suddenly: "Love me the way you loved Monique."

I look at her. "Who says I loved Monique?"

And then: Images that sail past of her lying on the table, uniformed skirt halfway to her neck, hair pulled back in a tight column.

When the taxi honks downstairs, her behind is sticky and shiny.

"It's a good thing I'm a flight attendant," she says. "If you ever get tired of me, I can always switch to British Airways."

When I stagger out to the toilet, my clothes smell like an extinguished campfire. I smoke too much.

It's only under the shower that I revive in a pocket of sound.

In the mornings I have trouble coming back to life; the present is as unreal as my dreams. Only gradually do the pounding drops make me start to feel something that resembles rain. It's as if I'm not capable of feeling, as if something is shut off inside me. As if, on my worst days, I'm an actor in someone else's dream.

It wasn't always like that. Once upon a time I approached everything with a clarity like new frost. I twirled sweet, girlish kisses out of curled-up, frightened tongues. I had scrapes and bruises and black, swollen eyes from endless street fights. My lungs felt translucent, and there was a taste of autumn in my mouth.

When I was small, I used to walk backward in the snow to fool the grown-ups. But new snow fell, and no one could see that I'd been there.

Last night, I was so drunk I don't remember what we said or did. But from the scratches on my back I know that Natasha's sharp claws wrote a message in my flesh.

A sound of dry cardboard as I open the carton flap. Whole milk. After the low-fat kind it's like drinking cream. I crumple up the carton and clear the rest of the table.

I call the paper. Ask for Stella. Mimi in Reception answers. "Did you take care of the bank?"

"Yes."

"Were you overdrawn?"

"You might call it that."

She connects me. Stella answers.

"The new search went a little better," she says. "I've just got to break it down. You only want the ones with connections to Los Angeles, right?"

"Yes, please."

I usually let Stella take care of my computer searches. She's an expert. We got her from International Computer Center; that was before they became InfoScan. She keeps saying I have to learn to do it myself, but I don't have the energy. There are over thirty thousand databases in the world. Just the thought of all the different intricate computer languages you need to get from one to another makes me dizzy. Stella says the hard part is finding the right databases. When I complain that they don't even speak in the same codes, she counters by saying that mothers don't bring up all their children in the same way either.

"I'm almost ready with a list for you. Hope there's something you can use," she says.

"When do you think you'll have it?"

"Soon. But I've got other things to do, too."

"I know."

High up in the clouds, Natasha will be serving food soon. Maybe, at this very moment, the last of the sperm is running down her leg. Or perhaps it's dried to a flake, as if from a closed wound.

Up there in God's heaven.

Under the pounding of the shower I review the events of last night. What really happened? Did I go too far? Did she see what I am? Did she see herself for the first time, or had she always known? If I hadn't gagged her, tied her hands behind her back, whispered filth into her ear, would she have known? Or does this mean that it's not really her? What did I say? What does God have to say about all this?

If the circumstances had been different . . .

There was the Thai girl I slept with. Was her poverty an excuse for prostitution? An explanation in itself? Of course I pitied her, or felt anger on her behalf. The unequal distribution of wealth. The social inequities. But could I have loved her? Wasn't what she did an essential part of who she was? And if you never see your beloved in extreme situations, does that mean that you don't know her?

Or do the circumstances excuse everything?

Natasha. What did I say to her? What did I promise? And whom am I trying to punish? Her? Myself?

God?

I straighten up the apartment and put the envelopes of photos back onto the shelf in my workroom. Dented and tarnished, the trophies stand like strange remnants of a distant past. Reminiscences of a lost youth filled with sports. Their brass and dull pewter seem oddly antiquated, as though they belong to a civilization long since vanished. Even though I've stopped polishing them, they served their purpose: they made my victories visible. Dr. Phillip agrees that they're important. Because, he says, it's always easier to get good results with people who have demonstrated that they can produce.

I often take refuge here. In my room. But tonight I feel so strangely tired.

My eyes fall on a box of Monique's school keepsakes that I found in our attic storage room under an old dresser. It also contains old letters and postcards that she sent me from all her travels. Underneath the letters I found the note: Jack Roth Pascal, Hotel Four Seasons, room 505. Words had been crossed out, as if she'd tried to erase them, and the paper was crumpled up as if it was unimportant, or very important. I don't know when it was written. There could be a thousand explanations: maybe I came home early one day, and she hastily hid the paper and then forgot about it. That would make it older than last March; Monique lived at Marianne's place all of March. It's impossible to know.

It fell into place. Jealousy makes everything fall into place. But who is Jack Roth Pascal? She didn't say.

According to Dr. Phillip, there are two kinds of mourning: the mourning that finds release in tears and commiseration, and *my* kind. Huge, dark, repressed.

But he's still unsure.

"Usually the worst part is the uncertainty. But you *know*."

Uncertainty. Is that it? Is it a question of assigning a face to Jack Roth Pascal? Certainty. That he's the face in the picture. But is that all? Or is it a question of wanting to rip off that face?

I take the box of old letters into the living room. I read, but there's nothing about a joint account or secret rendezvous. Was that who he was? Her lover? Jack Roth Pascal.

Like thread basted loosely across the paper, the words stand unfinished: tight little messages, touching scribbles from an uncertain, milk-white hand. In places the ink has faded, like peeling light-blue paint. The sun has yellowed the paper; it's brittle, like autumn leaves curling up in yellow, twisted death paroxysms. Or are they merely curled up on sleep? The other letters in the box are meaningless. Nothing to decipher or decode, no solved mysteries. But they have sentimental value, like found amber—the tears of trees or clotted blood. Only when it's washed ashore on a distant beach a thousand years from now will it be valuable. Right now it's worthless. Like the swollen bank account. There is only uncertainty. Nothing more.

I pick up the telephone and call Marianne.

"I've got to know more."

She sighs. "Martin, don't you think you ought to let the police take care of it?"

"They still think I did it."

"But you've got your witness," she says.

My witness, yes. I take the telephone over to the bay window and look across the street. She isn't there. Right after they dropped the charges against me, I wondered who "saw" me. I tried to pump Inspector Klinker, but he wasn't talking.

"Molberg, you know perfectly well that I can't discuss the case."

"But I'm her fiancé."

"Exactly."

They questioned her circle of acquaintances. "That's where we usually find the perpetrator," Klinker said without suggesting that he'd crossed me off the list of suspects. The interrogation, the humiliation!

When my witness finally appeared, they made no apologies, offered no explanations. At least they stopped leaking details to the press, one of which was especially interesting.

"But we don't feel that it has any relevance now. And I thought you'd rather be spared."

"Am I supposed to be grateful?"

The only thing I could figure out was that my witness had to be the young woman across the street. She was there. She saw me. But as far as I could remember, I'd had the blinds drawn all evening. Memory often plays tricks. Especially on witnesses. It's incredible how few details we remember. As if we simply weren't there. Maybe my memory is faulty too, but it occurred to me that it might have been a lapse in her memory that furnished me with an alibi. Maybe I opened the blinds when I heard the sirens. Maybe she went to the window too, curious about the sound. Maybe that was what made her think that the blinds had been open all night, that she'd seen me earlier in the apartment, that I'd been there all the time. I haven't had a chance to speak to her yet.

The street's empty now. A black Mazda stands in front of the entrance to her building. I don't know if it's the same car.

Women hurry in and out of the shops with single-minded determination. Looking at them prosaically, you know that they're just salesgirls in fashionable boutiques, but they could also be highly paid mannequins, tanned by the camera's glare. The staggering wealth that has flowed into the neighborhood in recent years—and that shamelessly calls attention to itself—arouses no social indignation or resentment. We just watch it happening.

"There must be something more. She must have been seeing someone."

"She wasn't."

"She lived with you for a month, Marianne. Did the two of you sleep in the same room?"

"No, she slept in the living room. But she was here every night."

"There *must* have been someone else."

"There *wasn't*."

"Who was she supposed to see that day?"

"I don't know, Martin. She was hard to talk to. I think she was afraid."

"Afraid?"

She sighs. "If there was someone else, she would have said so. She didn't."

"Why didn't she want to see me?"

"I don't know, Martin. I just don't know. She didn't say. She wouldn't talk about it at all."

Two men appear in the street below. They stroll up to the building across the street; one of them unlocks the front door. They say good-bye to each other, and the other continues down the street.

"You're going to drive yourself crazy thinking about it, Martin. Let the police handle it."

"But there must be something else. Can't you come up with anything?"

She thinks for a while.

"The only thing is the package."

"The package?"

"One day a package arrived for her. A book or something. I don't know what it was. I wondered about it, because no one knew she was living here. You didn't send her a package?"

"No. Where is it now?"

"I don't know. I did look for it, but I can't find it."

"Who did it come from? Did it have anything written on it?"

She sighs. "Probably. But I don't remember. I had no idea it was important. I thought it probably came from you."

On the street the second man comes strolling back again. He passes the building and disappears again. A young man in an unusually large gray coat positions himself on the sidewalk across the street, his collar carefully turned up around his face. He looks up in this direction, as if he suddenly sees me. Then he hurries down the street.

I sit on the sofa for a moment, then call Klinker.

"How is the case coming along?" I ask.

"The case?"

"Why don't you just admit you're not working on it anymore?"

"We're still investigating."

"What?"

"All relevant leads."

"That point to me?"

"Not necessarily."

"But you still think it's me, right?"

"I can't discuss that with you, Molberg. You know that."

"Why do you assume I did it?"

"We don't assume anything at all."

"Then make some assumptions!" I say, and slam down the receiver.

I break off half a Dexedrine and swallow it. Then pack up the photographs and letters and put them back in the study.

A vague feeling comes over me, a vague suspicion. Anyone who's ever tried to cover his tracks knows how hard it is; there's always a small detail one forgets. I start in the kitchen. I photograph the rest of the apartment: the furniture from different angles, the bookshelves, one shelf at a time. Finally each of the ten photo envelopes in the box in the study. I put the box back on the shelf.

I look for the key to the attic storage room and bring the photograph along. Up the narrow staircase, the sun is shining through the small windows, making neat squares on the steps.

The attic is dark. I unlock the padlock to the storage area. The room is a narrow, totally dark corridor except for what light seeps through the woodwork under the roof. The wall to the left is lined with boxes. I'm about to pull the lid off one when the hall light suddenly goes out. I didn't press the timer switch hard enough. On my way out I stop; the hallway floor creaks. I freeze. The door's open. I think I hear someone breathing. Very carefully I feel my way in the dark and edge the lid off, keeping an eye on the door. Finally I push the photograph down into the box, replace the lid, and turn around. Groping for shelves and boxes, I find my way back to the door. Carefully I poke my head out past the doorjamb. No one's there. I turn on the light. No one. I go back to the box and take out the photograph again. From now on this photograph is not leaving my sight.

Back in the apartment I dress, lock the door and check it to make sure. I walk down to the photo shop and turn in the film.

The photo dealer, a snorting man with a walrus mustache, looks at his watch, panting heavily.

"Is next week early enough?"

"Next week is fine."

I call Stella. She's gone. Then I call Lindvig.

"I have something I want you to see. Do you have time?"

"Yes. What's the matter? You don't sound so good," he says.

"I think I'm going crazy."

"Crazy about whom?"

Chapter Nine

I'm the one who says computers will poison our lives. Lindvig smiles knowingly.

"You sound like our parents when they couldn't stand rock 'n' roll."

"It's not the same thing," I say.

"It's exactly the same thing. Look at this."

He's sitting at the keyboard, a magician before a screen. Strange numbers scroll up and down with lightning speed. Curves crackle and colorful bands dance like small Milky Ways on his screen.

"What happened to the old one?"

He nods toward his workroom. There was something human about his old IBM. Lindvig's password was "Erection." But he'd programmed it with an extra security step: when it came back and asked, "Why should I let you in?" the next password was, "Because I turn you on."

The new machine looks like the old one, but it's much more powerful, says Lindvig.

"Object-programming," he informs me. "We've got some new software."

"You put it in the living room!" I say indignantly.

"Do you realize how much it cost me?"

"It's a toy."

"Let me tell you something, Molberg. Ten years ago the programs required about 100,000 lines of codes. Now it's over a million. In ten years it'll have passed ten million. I have to keep up with everyone else."

"I don't get it."

"Yes, you do. You just don't want to. Before, a person had to start from scratch every time he wanted to write a new program. There's no more time for that, and it isn't necessary either. Now I can handle a big project of up to ten million lines of program codes with only 200,000 lines."

We're two representatives of a generation who have no common frame of reference. Lindvig does a good job at DataCentral; but now his work has invaded his home, too. I'm not against the new technology; I merely reserve judgment. That's the difference between us. Lindvig supports it unconditionally, I remain skeptical.

"Computers haven't made anything happen any faster."

"That's simply not true."

"That's what all the statistics say."

He's typing.

"I've just got to finish this up, then I'll be right with you." He keeps typing. "It's really only a question of time and standards. As soon as we're all connected in networks, you'll see the advantages."

"We'll be able to speak across borders."

"Precisely," he says.

"And exchange data without regard to race or religion?"

He nods.

"We'll be close to strangers and cut off from those closest to us."

"Oh, shut up," he says.

Computers. Already there are tired, worn-out models. An earlier generation just like our own. Amazing what they're capable of; also amazing what they can't do. They're like children—in the crawling stage.

"Computers are stupid."

"You ought to read something about neural networks."

Lindvig and I see each other a good deal, but I don't really know him very well. At one point we moved in the same circles, and while we researched our TV project, I made diligent use of him as a background source. But we're not close. Something's missing. Maybe it's that you rarely develop lifelong friendships later in life. The foundation is missing, the fact that you've known each other since you were kids, that you share a common past. We spend time together, but we're not close friends.

The few times he met Monique, it was obvious that what he appreciated most was her sense of order. Lindvig's home is always impeccable. He likes clean lines: simple, spare, but expensive designer furniture; rich colors. And only nondeciduous plants.

With his windblown, well-groomed, shiny hair, his sparkling blue eyes, his white teeth, his glistening, manicured nails, he sits there, typing efficiently at the computer. They're completely at ease with each other. He's learned its language and speaks it fluently.

Maybe he and I are just too different. He has a sunny disposition and direct access to his feelings. He can be quite irresistible, and in a way I envy him. Lindvig defined himself a long time ago. His sexuality. He knows what he is. And because he knows what he is, he knows what he feels. He never seems to have any doubts about the big things: life, the meaning of it all, love. Or maybe he never thinks about them. While I do and know nothing.

Why can't I do as he does? And everybody else as well. Simplify myself so that contradictions never arise. Uncertainty. Doubt.

I don't know anyone who can fall in love the way Lindvig can. With magnificent abandon, he throws himself into one grand calamity after another, always taking remarkable pleasure even in defeat. Maybe that's why minorities have a passionate expression in their eyes, even when they talk about their worst troubles. When they've defined themselves, they've also defined their pain. And it's easier to deal with well-defined pain, however horrible, than with invisible suffering.

Lindvig has no father; that's why he is the way he is. Or that's how Dr. Phillip would see it. And I became a journalist to satisfy *my* father, who probably became what he is to satisfy *his*. Trace the guilt back endlessly in time. And the crime becomes symbolic. Not what it seems. Really no one's guilty, but still I'm the one stuck with the responsibility. Judgment is passed on everyone, but it doesn't seem to have to be expiated. Maybe the guilt is punishment enough.

Ever since I was little, I've known about expectations. Nothing was ever good enough. Maybe my restlessness can be explained by the need for calm, which always had to be gained through praise. Insufferable weakness was denied. Gradually the restlessness metamorphosed into a chronic headache, a pain in a forehead that in the end felt no fear. Feelings froze until rigidity became stylized—a frozen, mannered style that pretended to a harmony no deeper than the words that created it.

How Dr. Phillip would revel in all this! But he's not going to get the chance. Even though all my accomplishments may have originated in my father's coldness, I won't let Dr. Phillip off the hook: let him rummage around in all his definitions and theories, one of which is that it's easier to get good results with a neurotic patient who's an achiever.

In Lindvig's world, murky concepts like guilt and responsibility don't exist. Only pure, constant, extreme passions. Lindvig is a connoisseur of the pleasures of living, and all his life he's had everything handed to him on a silver platter. His apartment—all the rooms have direct views of the harbor—was given to him by a wealthy lover, who never, even after Lindvig ended the relationship, could forget him. For a few years the man continued to send lavish gifts and large sums of money, until Lindvig made it clear beyond any doubt that the two of them were through. Then the poor wretch took his life—and willed his entire fortune to Lindvig, who ever since has done everything in his power to squander it.

"How was Los Angeles? Tell me about it. Coffee?" he says, getting up and signaling me to follow him.

While he arranges cups and cakes and coffee on a tray, he listens distractedly. Compared to Lindvig's escapades, Los Angeles doesn't sound like much, and as usual I wonder if he's even capable of working up any real interest in *my* affairs.

We return to the living room and sit down. Lindvig pours the coffee.

"So you *did* meet someone?"

"In a manner of speaking."

"But how do you *feel* about her?" he asks.

"How do I feel? I don't really know," I say.

"And yet you sleep with each other? I'm shocked."

"I just met her. You make it sound as if that's all we do together."

He smiles. "What else do you do?"

"Nothing. I just met her."

He smiles.

Shocked. Of course he's not shocked. But, as always, if you don't feel immediate and totally uncontrollable passion, Lindvig wheels out the heavy moral artillery. Perhaps it's a result of the self-righteous condemnation which I've noticed he often uses in his own favor and which makes it possible for him to justify all the quick flings he excels at. No one could ever accuse him of merely satisfying a narrow biological need, for whenever he talks about a new relationship, he always calls forth visions of great love, the one true love.

"If you don't know what you feel, then why do you sleep with her?" he asks, still scandalized.

"I don't know," I say. "I suppose she validates me."

That makes him perk up his ears.

"And what exactly is she validating?" He grins. His crafty grin.

"Maybe we're just comforting each other," I say, and give him a somewhat sugary description of certain similarities she has to Monique. Or maybe I merely remind Natasha of a boyfriend *she* can't forget. But Lindvig finds this so pathetic that he's about to throw up. Then he gets serious.

"I know how you must feel," he says.

"Actually, I don't think you do."

"Then why don't you talk about it?"

"What do you mean?"

"Say what you feel. About what happened to Monique."

"I don't feel anything."

"You will," he says.

"That's what everyone says."

I let my eyes sweep his bookcases. Films. Videos. Film and computers: they fill up his life. He has hundreds, maybe even thousands. He once told me that even his attic is packed with film. He has everything under the sun: regular feature films, of course, both the ones he's bought and, more often, pirated copies purchased through his secret film-studio contacts. Just like other hobbyists, Lindvig has refined and specialized his selection of curios, such as cuts of the only televised electric-chair execution; the Zapruder footage of Kennedy which he got long before the movie *JFK;* countless porn movies, the contents of which I don't even dare inquire about; illegal snuff movies; catastrophe tapes, which are among the crown jewels of his collection and in which one horror succeeds another. Imperceptibly, without looking back, Lindvig has entered a new phase of his life.

While we drink coffee in the living room, we watch some gory videos from Kuwait during the Iraqi occupation—blurred, grainy footage of three women being raped and tortured by what look like Iraqi soldiers. According to Lindvig, they're amateur tapes smuggled from Spain. At the end, one of the women has her throat slit with a sheet of paper.

Lindvig owns miles of this kind of footage. Where he gets it and from whom, no one knows. A lot of it he's taped right off the

TV, but there are things I don't even want to know the origin of.

We sprawl on his couch drinking coffee while images from the Challenger tragedy float silently across the screen. A great display of fireworks explodes and shakes the picture; fire, and a tail of smoke pour out into the blue air like a drop of milk in a mug of tea.

"Do you realize what awful quality that picture has?" he says dully. "Isn't it incredible that we have to *look at* that kind of thing?"

I sit watching him for a while. He never seems to tire of these images. What do they mean to him? I don't know his real thoughts, his real longings, or the loss in his past that demands to be fed by these monstrous pictures.

"Lindvig, you'd tell me if Monique had someone else, wouldn't you?"

He turns his face.

"Why do you say that?"

I shrug. "Maybe to avoid some kind of misplaced sense of loyalty?"

"Monique didn't have someone else," he says. "Not as far as I know, anyway."

I pull out the photo.

"What is it?" He sits up.

"The question is: Who is it?"

"Monique?"

"Obviously. But who is he?"

"I don't know."

"No one does."

"Did you show it to the police?"

"No."

"Why not?"

"They still think I did it. What do you suppose they'll think if I show them this?"

"Do you know who he is?"

"I think his name is Jack Roth Pascal. Possibly Jacob Roth Pascal."

"But if you know his name, I suppose you know who he is?"

"No, I have no idea."

He studies it for a while. "It's blurred. But the murder was in all the papers, so why hasn't he come forward?"

"The newspaper photos were old. Maybe he didn't recognize her."

"Or maybe he did it."

"Maybe."

"Where did you get the photo?"

"From Marianne. Monique lived with her at the end."

"You never told me that."

"I don't know what was going on. It was all a mess. Monique wouldn't talk about it."

"Maybe she did have someone else. When was the picture taken?"

"That's what's so strange. If she'd just fallen in love. But she hadn't. Marianne insists that she hadn't."

He listens thoughtfully.

"So maybe this is the guy who did it?"

I nod. "If Monique didn't tell Marianne," I say, "maybe there wasn't any new guy. But then who is he?"

"Was she mixed up in something? Could she have been blackmailed?"

"I don't know."

"Where was it taken?"

"In a hotel in Los Angeles."

"Jack Roth Pascal, you say. Is he American?"

"Perhaps."

"Well, there's no question of what's going on in the picture," he says.

"That's what's so strange. Why would she save it? Look at it! It's not the kind of picture you'd save."

He shakes his head.

"But she did," I say. "She kept it in a book at Marianne's house. Why would she do that if she wanted to get rid of it? And if I tell you that I've just been told by the bank that in March Monique deposited two million crowns in an account, what would you think then?"

"I'm not sure you want to hear."

"Tell me."

"They're making love. But they don't love each other. They're together, but they didn't have an affair. I'm thinking of pornography, Molberg. That's all I can come up with."

"Who do we know who knows something about pornography?"

Chapter Ten

"I've been saving up," she says.

Amazed, I stare at the expensive TV, the antique harpsichord, and the sterling silver candelabra in her apartment.

"Sit down for a while. I'm not quite ready."

She leaves the room to finish dressing. Those black stocking-covered, gold-flecked legs. I can't keep my eyes off them.

In a little while she's back.

"Shall we?" she says.

We leave.

I'm wondering how far *she* would go. If she would ever allow a picture like that to be taken. Some women make a living that way. Men too.

Everything's so disconnected. Her face with its polite smile. Her impeccable manners, impeccable facade. And underneath, her lust. As we sit in the restaurant, I wonder what her limits are. I picture the chef's hand on the inside of her thigh, her wet crotch and rumpled clothes as he thrusts into her on the counter in the back room. But I can't fathom it. I can't picture Monique actually being in that situation.

I remember a summer's day with Monique. After a trip to the beach: the high sun. A weekend at Kullen in Sweden in her parents' boat. We drifted up against the rocks, and as always, our backs got the late afternoon sun.

When we got home, she was brown and disturbingly beautiful. On little, red-painted toes, she slinked up behind me, her blond hair pulled up into a taut, shiny ponytail. She pressed herself against me, silently, stalkingly. The skin on my back was dust-dry and drank up almost all the oil her smooth hands rubbed on it, the citrus oil disappearing as though into blotting paper.

"Rub it too?" I said, pulling down my pants.

"No!" She struck her mouth with her hand.

"But it wants to feel soft too . . ."

"Hopefully not," she said quietly. Then giggled.

That puzzling little grin. And I thought: I don't know her at all. What is she like when she's with other people? I only know her as an extension of myself.

Things we never would have thought possible in our youth, would have rejected as grotesque, are no longer so improbable. There's an inherent modesty in us all that disappears over the years. There are things we never would have done that we no longer rule out. I've thought of this in connection with my parents. Things we've never spoken of, words I've never had in my mouth around them, situations we've never discussed—I've written about in the newspaper. I wonder if they ever read it, and what they think. Did something grow in Monique that I didn't see? Something I didn't want to see?

I've never been able to fathom it. To see a person you know

transformed into a greedy or whimpering creature, reduced to skin and smells. To see yourself panting heavily. I've raped women in my life, but I've never been prosecuted for it. Girls who didn't want to; girls who did want to, but at first didn't; girls who afterward protested so unconvincingly that it was clear that even if all through it—and even afterwards—they insisted that they hadn't wanted to, they had. I remember a period of my life when I got so sick of the whole thing that I totally lost my desire and coasted on automatic. One night in a drunken stupor with some nameless woman, afterwards I heard her sigh and make a remark intended to wound:

"That's the first time I felt absolutely nothing."

I was cold as ice. "Who says you're supposed to feel something?"

Natasha smiles across the table.

"What are you thinking about?" she asks.

"You."

We're eating foie gras as an appetizer. Foie gras d'oie. Monique loved foie gras. Foie gras, French wines, classical music. She had refined tastes.

The taste of foie gras d'oie is delicate and light. The consistency of the meat of the finest fruits—rose-colored with a swirl of color a half tone darker. Like skin and its shadows.

"You know how they make it, don't you?" I say.

Natasha nods and smiles.

"Macabre, isn't it?"

They've cut the block of pâté into slices with a warm knife, but haven't separated them: the slices lean against each other on the plate. The Périgord truffles are as large as fingernails and taste like rarefied nut meat. We drink Sauterne.

The tablecloth is made up of peach-colored designs, with matching ribbons tied to the three flowers that twine themselves, crescent-moonlike, around the white plates. Peaches have been cut in swirls and arranged next to the foie gras as decoration, with a few raspberries and a sprinkling of greens. Golden toasted bread rests under a white lace napkin.

She's like the food. Light, and yet black and mysterious like the truffles, and with the same foreign taste. As I sit watching her, I realize that what I said to Lindvig about my conflicting feelings for her is actually true. Sitting there in her black dress, her full, grooved lips the same blue-black color as the truffle slices, she absorbs all light around herself, as though she spreads a veil of darkness over her surroundings. One is drawn magnetically to the edges of the shadow, but then one becomes wary.

I think about the black windowpane on the other side of the street and wonder how far the police will go. Will they assign a man whose only job is to keep an eye on Molberg, whose fiancée so violently lost her life? Are they waiting for Molberg to go on a two-million-crown spending spree, the acquisition of which money was his motive? Does Natasha work for the police? Is that what's really happening?

Natasha is different from Monique. It's as though her body is struggling to step into the same light and easy grace as Monique's, but then keeps being forced into a darkness, either its own shadow or a shadow thrown over it. Room 505. I saw her, but I didn't actually see her go in there. Not for sure.

Her black crêpe de Chine dress hugs her body. On the sleeves little puffs of curly taffeta stick out, and her legs shimmer in black and gold. Her mouth is grooved and fruitlike: before she licks it, it's bluish red, like elderberry. From her ears dangle a pair of gold rings that end in small curlicues, and I notice the Cartier watch like a streak of gold on her wrist.

"Bangkok," she says. "But it's a good imitation." For a moment I sit thinking: I know how to spot a fake Rolex but have forgotten how to tell a real Cartier from an imitation.

"I always heard that you can't trust a reporter," she says.

"Can you trust a flight attendant?"

She laughs. "Why don't you write a novel? Don't all reporters dream of writing a novel?"

"No," I say.

She smiles.

There's something youthfully unfinished about her face—a teasing glint in her eyes you can't be sure of, but at the same time she's steady as a sphinx. She crosses her legs, one tight, pointy leg twisted over the other like the stinger of a poisonous insect.

"Why don't you write a novel about the lost love of your life?" she says.

"Monique?"

"Tell me about her. Was it all raw passion? Do you still cry yourself to sleep thinking of her?"

"If you don't mind, I'd rather not."

"Did she break your heart?" she says, smiling. I can't believe she hasn't read about it. I watch her for a while. She's not cruel. It can't just be to hurt me that she says it. It can't possibly be. She simply doesn't know. She cannot know.

I excuse myself and go to the bathroom. On my way down the stairs my legs fold under me, and I almost slide the rest of the way, one arm clutching the railing. All I have are some Thorazines and one and a half Dexamyl. I drink some water and swallow the Dexamyl and a Thorazine, then take another half Thorazine so I won't become too manic. I splash some water in my face and stand holding on to the sink, staring into the running, swirling water. The water disappears down the drain in gurgling spirals. I dry my face and walk back up.

She sits smoking a cigarette. Her shoe gently seesaws at the end of her foot. Under the stocking you can just make out the little teasing Y where the foot disappears into the toe of the shoe.

A moment later I feel her foot under the table.

"Usually I'm a nice girl," she grins.

There are mostly couples in the restaurant. Diagonally across from us a very quiet middle-aged couple are eating soup. Solemnly, almost as though the plates are sacred, they dip their spoons so silently that it seems they're eating air. Farther away, halfway hidden behind a palmette, its stony leaves protruding from the column, a younger couple eat cautiously, as though they think the bill will be smaller that way. At the very end of the room, two young couples are talking to each other across the tables. When we finish our main course, a noisy party appears at the entrance. Immediately I see Jan Borris. The people are shown to a table next to the two sociable couples at the other end, but Borris, squinting and swaying, sees me and comes over. I politely introduce him to Natasha, partly to avoid an embarrassing scene, but my only thought is that his presence defiles the place. It takes no time to see how drunk he and his companions are: the other three people in his party head for their table, the women in black crotch-length dresses and stockings, giggling and shrieking.

"They're up to their asses in money," Borris says. "One of them"—he turns, about to lose his balance—"that one,"—he points—"Nicole, she thinks she can become a movie star if only she can get her picture in the paper."

"Then what's she doing here with you?" I say.

"You think you're such hot shit," he says. "How the hell did you do it?" He grabs the chair to keep his balance.

"Well, you did give me the name of his agent."

He pushes down his face next to mine.

"Don't you think I know what a bitch it is just to get hold of *him*?"

There's a thump followed by the sound of breaking glass and china from the direction of Borris's loud friend. One of the women has fallen, pulling the tablecloth almost to the floor. After a moment's silence both women explode with laughter. A waiter heads toward them, but Borris stops him.

"I'll take care of that. We'll pay for everything. She'll pay, I mean."

"She'll go far," I say, but he doesn't hear me.

"Who was that?" Natasha says incredulously.

"Just an idiot."

Our coffee arrives.

"What were you really doing in Los Angeles?" she asks.

I light a cigarette.

"I had an interview. With Jack Nicholson."

She smiles.

"What did he ask you about?"

I smile at her.

"And," I say, "I was also looking for a man."

"Who?"

"A man called Jack Pascal. Jack Roth Pascal."

I try to read her reaction. There's nothing to read.

"Is he an actor too?"

"I don't know. I don't know much about him."

"Then why were you looking for him?"

"Why do you think?"

She shrugs. "How would I know?"

I don't know what else to say. Sipping our coffee, we sit for a while in silence.

"You ask a lot of questions," I say.

"You don't *say* a lot."

"Touché."

As the waiter passes, I ask for the bill. I give him my card, and he returns quickly with the receipt.

"I thought reporters were used to questions."

"Yes, to asking them. Shall we go?" I say.

"Commercials!" we hear from Borris's friend. "I'm not going to be in any fucking commercials."

We stroll silently along the lakes. The air is warm. May. Soft, dark-green smells waft past under the trees by the bridges. Leaf-boats float on the surface of the water among hairy tufts of silkweed.

I wonder if the meeting with Borris has made her uncomfortable. Did I say something wrong? Does she know Jack Roth Pascal? And I think about the bank account. Where did Monique get all that money?

Spires and towers of the city's roofscape cut blackly into the pale evening sky. The tall gables with their pinnacles and the floodlit domes make the houses of the city look like fairy-tale castles. Lower down, the grotesque silhouettes of occasional gargoyles hang on the parapets of buildings.

For a moment I see this as the true face of the city. A haggard head, a distorted beauty. I'm sorry I didn't stuff my pockets with Dexedrines.

In Tivoli we sit in the pavilion with the red and blue lights by the slow-moving boats. We get drunk. Later, as we go from the pavilion to the fountains and the fireworks display, the two are suddenly in front of us. Natasha is giggling and tipsy, her black dress flapping around her and a pink brush of cotton candy in her hand. My hair is tousled and sweaty, my eyes red. It's Monique's parents.

Her father has regained his color, but with a grim expression he pulls me away from Natasha. Monique's mother is working on a pale smile.

"How about showing a little common decency?" he says angrily, gripping the sleeve of my jacket.

"What do you mean?" I say.

"She's dead! Can't you get that through your head?"

I tear myself free, my head swimming. Furiously I push my face close to his.

"*Who* exactly is dead?"

I walk off.

He stands silently.

Monique's mother attempts another soothing smile, but I grab Natasha's arm.

"Come on, we're going," I say, putting my arm through hers.

"Who was that?" she whispers as we head down the path. Monique's mother stands forlorn and alone in the dark.

"Just an idiot," I say.

"You seem to know a lot of idiots," she says, but I don't answer.

We don't make love. Only later that night do we talk to each other.

While Natasha sleeps silently in the bedroom, I open the bay window. Outside, a fine mist fills the air.

Maybe I ought to call Dr. Phillip. Then again, maybe I ought to go back to Natasha now that I don't feel so dizzy. Thank goodness we have each other, Natasha and I. I keep repeating this to myself, trying to warm myself by the thought.

On the street below, a pair of lovers stroll slowly in the rain. Under the street lamp craning its neck above them, they stop and kiss. In the sleepy lamplight they look like two air-brushed beauties. They must be young; only young people kiss so calmly in the rain.

I look at the dark window of the young woman's apartment, then at the building next door with its dark glass staring emptily into the night.

Suddenly I smile at the thought of a story Natasha told me about when she worked at a freshwater biology institute in Hillerod. Her job was to determine the sexual identity of beach fleas.

"You're easier," was what she said.

But not tonight.

She didn't say anything, just lay there with her nails scratching gently between my legs. Then she gave up. Not to hurt her feelings, I told her it had happened before.

When we went to sleep, she silently crawled under the comforter.

As I stand by the window, I can feel her like a shadow in the doorway behind me, and when I turn around, I feel a tender pull in my gut as I see her standing there stretching and yawning. She rubs her eyes.

"What are you doing?" she asks quietly.

"Thinking . . ."

I turn back and lean on the windowsill. The young couple are gone.

"There are people who have nowhere to live, and still there are empty apartments. There's nothing as sick as empty apartments."

Natasha comes over and stands behind me. She rests her face on my back and puts her arms around me.

"Well, at least they keep it well. The windows sparkle," she says.

"So do the eyes of insects."

She kisses my back.

"Don't think about it anymore," she says.

"That's not what I'm thinking about."

I turn and kiss her. She sighs gently. I force her backward onto the rug. Her hair spreads out in soft curly waves.

She protests weakly and tries to get up.

"I don't want to," she says. "Not now."

But I tighten my grip on her wrists, holding them together above her head with one hand while I pull off her panties with the other.

Eyes frightened, she tries to wriggle loose, but I hold her tightly. Slowly she relaxes, her head bending backward, her hands opening.

We make love aggressively, almost as if we're directing our anger against what we're doing.

Firmly gripping her neck, for a second I see Monique before me and I press, but she's no longer scared.

"More," she says. "More . . ."

When I finally fall asleep, I have a dream that I've had ever since I was a boy. A nightmare. As I'm trying to go to sleep in the dark, a woman is leaning over me. She smiles and pushes the comforter up around my chin as though she's trying to tuck me in. But suddenly she tightens it around my neck and tries to strangle me.

Soaked in sweat, I wake up, but Natasha is the one who's screaming. She sits upright next to me, her hair wet, staring out into the room. I fold her into my arms, and slowly she calms down.

"I must have had too much to drink. I never have nightmares."

"I do," I say. Slowly we drift back into the pillows, but I can't go back to sleep.

Then I remember. In one movement, I scoop up her watch on the bedside table and bring it to the kitchen. There I place it on the counter, reach for a glass in the cabinet, and turn on the faucet. While the water's running, I fold a dish towel around the glass and knock off the bottom. Then I study the watch through the bottom of the glass. On an original Cartier the second hand floats instead of jerks, and the name is written in tiny letters between the numbers six and seven. Not so on copies.

I turn off the light, go back inside, return the watch to the night table, and lie down. Why would anyone lie themselves *poorer* than they are?

I toss and turn but can't fall back to sleep. Finally I get up again, walk back into the living room, and pour myself a big vodka. I break a Unisom into halves and swallow them both. I'm tired but can't sleep. I walk over to the bay window, then back to the couch. The TV images float by soundlessly. I click around to all the stations of the world. Most of them show nothing but test patterns.

Light in itself can't be seen, but without it we'd see nothing. TV *is* light: it's the only medium that emits light; that's the secret of our fascination with it. The light, some say, creates a condition reminiscent of hypnosis. An outside signal controls the electronic beam which, at great speed, zigzags across our screen. As we watch, our reception is bombarded by periodic signals that create a kind of synchronization of alpha, beta, and delta rays, resembling the brain's own delta waves. We tune in.

I get up, go to the bay window, and open the blinds. The young woman's apartment is dark. For a long time I stand there staring at nothing. At one point, when I turn my head, I think I see a flash of light. I think it's in the empty apartment. Then I decide I must be so tired that I'm seeing things and make up my mind to go back to bed. Careful not to wake her, I lie down and think about the enormous trust we show when we lie so close to each other. We're so vulnerable when we sleep; we could kill each other in an instant.

Slowly I sink back into sleep. Natasha's face is staring at me when I wake up.

"You look so sweet when you're sleeping," she says.

"I am sweet," I say, "when I'm sleeping."

Chapter Eleven

With Natasha my body finally begins to acknowledge some of the thoughts that until now have only hovered around it as possibilities.

I feel that I'm collapsing, melting. There's a vacuum in my gut, I am like an insect that has just lost its stinger. And when my sperm silently falls on her uniform, tiny tears push out of my eyes the way pain does after a slap on the face.

Once upon a time—before Monique—I was afraid of casual love. I was restless, tired of meaningless relationships. I needed a woman who wanted to be loved, but who needed it just a little less than I did, so that she dared to show it. I don't really know if that's true. Perhaps love wasn't what I needed at all.

With Monique, love died. Or perhaps it died a long time before. On some night that's already forgotten. Perhaps it never got a chance. Perhaps it never had a chance. Perhaps it still doesn't.

With Natasha it's all been so messy. An accidental meeting in an airport on the other side of the world, a bit of fondling in a plane, and then a promise to call. Did I make it happen? I don't know. When I think of Natasha, I think mostly of her body. And about what she was doing in that hotel.

"Take me right here," she whispers.

Seen from the outside, the apartment must look like a puppet theater whose stage manager can't quite decide whether or not to start the show. Since I'm aware that people may be looking, I don't want them to see my private life. But Natasha insists. We're standing in the bay window. I shut the venetian blinds; she opens them again.

"It's much sexier this way," she says firmly, pulling me in front of the window. She stretches her arms, and her breasts become as flat as a boy's when she pulls her uniform jacket over her head.

"Come," she says, unzipping my pants. Then drops and surrounds my penis with a soft, wet, embracing tongue.

"Good baby. Good baby," she whispers.

I feel sick. Dragging myself to the couch in the living room, I lie under the down comforter with a gravelly exhaustion in my face and a small, thumping pain in my forehead. I take a Sulpril, but I still feel jumpy.

Leafing through the newspaper, all I can look at are the pictures.

When I feel this way, I try not to go out on the street, because the deformed, distorted faces of friends get superimposed on perfect strangers. My whole body's restless, and I feel an insect-like prickling under my skin. I've got to get hold of myself.

The young woman across the street is washing herself in the kitchen, one part at a time, top to bottom. When she splashes water up into her armpits, her breasts shiver. Not everyone has a bathroom yet. Suddenly she looks directly over at me. Then she smiles.

Quickly I look away. In the building next door, the old lady has raised her arm. At first it looks as though she's waving, but then I see the threatening, clenched fist—the small, dry, clenched fist. The black windowpane of the first building looks like the eye of a cyclops. The young woman has disappeared.

Demonstratively I turn the page of the paper, shutting them out: a few young people are showing off the latest dance; the government is neck-and-neck with the opposition. In the gossip column a pair of new lovers are photographed with their heads so close together that they look like Siamese twins: maybe it's their first photograph together.

I can't bear to read the newspapers anymore. Yet another young woman has been found murdered, and as usual the description of the suspect is hopelessly vague. Is it only the murderer who's guilty? I'm never entirely sure until they've caught him. I don't know when this started, but inside my head I go over my own movements. I'm still not convinced. Do I get up in the middle of the night and commit ghastly crimes, crimes I can't recall?

I don't remember in clear pictures anymore—just in shifting images and dead ends.

"Aren't you afraid of growing old?" I once asked Lindvig.

"I'm afraid that I won't," he said.

They say that old people are wise. But isn't the real truth that old people get so senile that they don't remember what they know?

That's what I fear. Not death, but loss of memory. The final blackout.

I don't remember exactly what happened that night. Did some kind of monster in me suddenly decide to put its life in order? The scratch in the windowpane that wasn't there before. Did I throw something against the window? Was I alone? Or was Monique there too? And was she what I threw?

These days. Strangely unreal. Fluid. Maybe they could have been avoided. The Thorazines take the worst of the edge off, but still I have an uneasy feeling throughout my body when I drive into town. We circle like hungry sharks, hunting for parking spots. When I spot a young woman walking along with a set of keys, I glide up behind her. She turns around and I roll down the window:

"Are you going for a ride?"

"No thanks," she says, giggling, and quickly moves away. I don't have time to explain.

I pick up my film. With a tired sigh the overweight shopowner hands me the pictures. Then I go to the paper. In Reception they tell me Stella hasn't arrived yet.

Walking down the long corridors between office cubicles, I reach the central editorial room. Behind screens and partitions people are talking on the telephone; otherwise, the room's empty. Only Solker stands in the middle, one hand holding a receiver, the other typing at a computer keyboard.

"Just try to get her age. I don't want any more bullshit."

He goes back to the phone.

"What were you saying? . . . Just a minute . . . yeah, here it is: Owner Rapes Tenant. Well, at least that takes care of her rent for the month . . ."

In hot weather people are apathetic. With long, lazy gestures they take just a few big, sprawling notes on pads cluttered with doodles and drawings. TV screens pour their streams of pictures into the sun-filled room. A few reporters are scrolling long lists of news releases from AP and Reuters onto their screens, and in the dry, crackling air you can hear the layout artists' crisp keyboard-patter and perpetual clicks from the computer mice. There's a sense of peace in the room: dusty sunbeams float through the windows, making the large junglelike plants throw shadow screens across the wall.

I take the elevator upstairs and let myself into my office to read the papers. I get a cup of coffee from the vending machine and sit staring at the blue screen for a couple of hours. I'm still restless.

In our best moments we're sure that there's a truth hidden behind that screen, a truth even deeper than what our imaginations can conceive. But those moments are rare. And almost never happen anymore. This is where I work. I don't know why anymore. I haven't known for a long time; I ought to walk out the door and never come back. But I don't know where I'd go—or why.

None of us writes very well. None of us feels like trying. We don't have to. None of us explores anything in depth. None of us feels like it. It's not worth the trouble. No one cares.

Stella calls.

"I have the list for you."

"I'm on my way."

When I get to her office in the archives, she points to a pile of papers next to her. "There you are," she says.

I pick up the papers and study them.

"Did you find out anything else?" she says, continuing to work at her keyboard.

I shake my head.

"Don't you know what he does for a living? A name isn't much to go by."

"No, I'm sorry," I say. "Did we try *Dialogue?*"

"Some of them. Do you realize how many bases there are in *Dialogue?*"

"What about *Nexus?*"

"I've tried *Nexus.* He's neither quoted nor referred to in any newspapers, weeklies, or magazines. At least not in any of the leading ones."

"Perhaps he just didn't make it into the database."

"Martin, it's a total-text database. He isn't there."

"Is it just for the US?"

She shakes her head. "For the whole world."

"Does that mean that if he exists, he'll be in there?"

"*If* he exists."

I go home.

The attack hits me before I make it to the car. Overcome with dizziness, I have to steady myself against a wall before I can go on. In the last rays of the sun the floating, glittering chrome on the cars makes them seem almost alive, and I have the uncomfortable feeling that someone's following me, but when I turn around, no one's there.

In my car I discover that I'm out of Dexedrines. I run a red light because the face in the next car keeps staring at me. The face is like an iron-tight grip on my neck.

As I'm about to open the door, I hear someone shouting from across the street. It's the old lady. She's standing trancelike, hitting a parked car with her cane.

"Bastard!" she's shouting.

When I walk over to talk to her, she quickly goes into her building, shutting the front door behind her.

Everything seems bewitched, disjointed. Only when I'm back in my own apartment can I begin to calm down. I scour the bathroom for Thorazines, find half a Dexamyl in the kitchen cabinet and swallow it as fast as I can. Then I get a glass, some ice, and the bottle from the liquor cabinet, and collapse on the couch.

After the first searing swallow, the liquor spreads warmly under my skin. When the numbing effect sets in, everything becomes distant. In the glass the whiskey is like threads and spirals of melted gold. I doze.

Later I spread the photos out on the table and examine them one by one, walking around, comparing. I study the bookcase, the red chaise lounge with the plants behind it, the television, the shelf filled with videos, the CDs in the bookcase, vases, knickknacks, sofas, pillows. Mementos of Monique. Everything's as it's supposed to be. I go over the pictures room by room, pull out the box of photo envelopes and leaf through them too. In sections of ten envelopes I go through the whole box. The sequence is correct, but to be absolutely sure, I go over them one more time. That's when I discover the tiny telltale detail: the sequence is correct, but one of the envelopes was put back in the box the wrong way, the flap turned the wrong direction. Not that there's an actual order, but the picture I took of the arrangement isn't the same as it is now. Someone's taken the envelope out and replaced it backward. I sit there going over it for a long time, but there's no doubt. Even though I can't find any traces of a break-in, someone's been here. I check the front door for signs of a screwdriver or a chisel: nothing. I take a flash-light and go up to the attic to check. Nothing there either.

Back downstairs, I go over everything one more time, but only that envelope is a clue that someone's been here. Natasha? She was here. She saw where I put the photographs, but she didn't see that particular one. She doesn't know it exists. Or does she? It could have been her. While I was sleeping. The police? Is she working for the police? Or did the police let themselves in without a warrant? Or what about the dead woman's keys? Maybe someone made a copy, intending to come back later and clean out the place. Or to remove a clue. Or a note with a name attached. Or a photo.

I call up Klinker.

"Another break-in? What did they take?"

"Nothing."

"I see," he says.

"What did you do about the other break-in?"

"I assumed it wasn't too serious," he says.

"Isn't a break-in serious?"

"Yes, but the thieves didn't take anything."

"Who says they were thieves?"

"What do you mean?"

"Do the police have a copy of my key?"

"Why the hell do you think that?"

"Why do you keep suspecting me? I didn't do anything."

"Well, you're not completely innocent, Molberg."

"What's that supposed to mean?"

"I seem to remember something about drugs. And there is that business about a fight in a bar."

"It was only a fine," I say.

"Yes, but you paid it, so technically speaking you have a record."

I take a deep breath.

"Someone's following me. Why are you following me?"

He takes a deep breath. Then, in a cloying voice:

"Are you feeling persecuted, Molberg?"

I pour myself a tall drink, then pour another. In the bathroom I take out the bottle of Demerol, break a pill in half—it works faster that way—and swallow both halves.

Suddenly the woman across the street is waving at me. As in a dream I walk up to the window and wave back. Before, it would have seemed all wrong. Most likely it wouldn't have happened at all. Even now I don't know if it's really happening.

She undoes her dress and lets it fall. Puts a finger in her mouth and widens her eyes as though she's done something naughty. She walks around naked for a while. Maybe she's tidying up. I stand in the bay window, swaying and shaking my whiskey cold in the glass.

She disappears deep into the apartment, but a moment later she's back. She bends down provocatively and picks up the dress, her behind to the window. Then she turns to make sure I'm still there. She smiles. And that is all. Then she's gone.

The booze has made me sleepy, and I lie down to take a nap before going to see Dr. Phillip. A sense of physical well-being floods me, as in a shallow sleep with distant voices. It's more than that: the Demerol washing through me makes me feel that everything is all right. Once when I was young, I always felt that way: I took it for granted. Now I need chemicals to find the peace and comfort that used to be there naturally. By definition

I'm a junkie: junkies take Demerol when they've run out of everything else. I've run out of everything else.

There in his chair sits my mentor, tall, dark, with little eyes that narrow to insectlike slits behind his thick lenses. Dr. Phillip. In his apartment high above the roofs of the city.

I wish I could submit to his authority. It would give my life meaning. But as it is, I think it's me who gives his life meaning.

Digging, snooping, groping, scrutinizing, eating his way into a long-vanished past. Dr. Phillip fishes for symptoms. I rattle off whatever occurs to me.

"Dizziness, choking sensations, the shakes . . ." My eyes wander around the room. He's busily taking notes, scratching out symptoms on his little scrap of paper. Behind him are all his books, shelves sagging with books. So many thoughts. So much suffering.

". . . insomnia, headaches"—the episode with Natasha occurs to me—"and a bit of a potency problem . . ."

I get up and walk over to the window. Marvelous view from up here, an eagle's-eye view.

"Any restlessness?" he asks, but I don't hear him and he has to repeat it.

"Yes, restlessness too," I say.

I walk back and sit down.

"You don't hear voices, do you?"

I smile.

"Only yours."

Undoubtedly I've repressed lots of things, says Dr. Phillip.

"But we all do in order to go on."

My dizziness. Nausea. And now this temporary impotence.

"It might be because of the pills," he says.

I can't say that I have any faith in Dr. Phillip's ability to produce miracles. Usually, our conversations end in total sophistry.

He has the same unshakable faith in the past that the doctors have at the hospital. I don't. At least not in their almost sacred adoration of the word. The past is full of accusations, but it holds no answers. Perhaps that's too categorical. I just don't know.

"And you're still taking the Thorazines I prescribed?"

I nod, limply.

"But I'm running out."

He looks up. "That was fast."

"I dropped some in the toilet."

He shakes his head, about to start admonishing me, but I interrupt him.

"I know, I know, I'm just like someone with diabetes."

"And you're not taking any other medication?"

"No," I lie.

Dr. Phillip tells me that I think too much. That I intellectualize. Acute personality disorder, he believes. As he says this, his eyes roll, as they always do when he's offering a diagnosis.

Lindvig also says I think too much, but he says it only in fun, when he knows I'm not listening, when my eyes go blank. And he doesn't give it a name.

Before I met Monique, my mother always used to say that it was because I lived alone. "It's unnatural," she said. Teasingly, Lindvig asked what exactly she meant by unnatural. He never gives up. In a way, I appreciate that: maybe he thinks I'm not a totally lost cause.

Seen from the outside, my life must look pretty trying. Sometimes even desperate. I don't dare tell him about the latest episode with Natasha. I haven't told Lindvig about Dr. Phillip. I'm not sure why. Maybe it's my way of reducing myself. Lindvig has his ways, too. Or maybe it's just an excuse. Maybe Dr. Phillip is right that I'm pushing everyone away. He says it would be better if I could just let it all out. Get it all worked through. If I could just open up. But I never really tell him anything. Once in a while, when I manage to put some sentences together, he listens so intently that I get the feeling he's spying on me. I don't trust him.

"You ask a lot of questions."

"It's my job to listen," he says.

"For whom do you listen?"

He lets himself fall back into his chair.

"I'm worried about you, Mr. Molberg."

"You don't have to be."

"Why haven't you talked about the break-in?"

"What do you know about that?"

"The police called me. Inspector Klinker."

"What did you tell him?"

"That I can't discuss my patients with him."

"Why did Klinker call you?"

"For heaven's sake, Mr. Molberg, people are worried about you."

"Worried about or interested in?"

He sighs.

"Even if I were working for the police, what difference would it make?" he says. "Since you have nothing to hide."

"Are you so sure of that?"

"Listen, Mr. Molberg, your problem—or one of your problems—is that you think too much. Give yourself a break. Relax a little."

I think too much. I know it. Day in and day out. Endless broodings that go nowhere. Interminable questions that give rise only to more questions.

Perhaps that's why I loved Monique. Her simplicity, her sweet, droll expressions. Everything about her was so simple; she came to you as insistently as a dog with a nudging snout, crying when she was sad and laughing when she was happy. When she was taken by an idea, a little dream, a beautiful view, her mouth would fall open slightly and her eyes would take on an expression of deep concentration. I desired that simplicity, wanted to live inside it, be surrounded by it, hide in it. I wanted to be that simple myself.

But immediately the questions come back. Could I have enjoyed the simplicity if I'd really been that simple?

Dr. Phillip listens with rapt attention to my speculations about love—my infantile regression into a lost past.

"I believe we're a bit stuck here," he says.

"Up to our eyeballs," I say.

He smiles reassuringly.

"Don't worry," he says. "But I don't like that shifting symptomology."

"Neither do I."

"Don't worry," he says.

I don't like his repeating it.

Chapter Twelve

"For anxiety" reads the label on the pill container—the curiously hopeful poetry of chemicals. I hide it. We all have our handicaps, our small vices. Life starts by trying to kill us; we have to take something against it.

Along the way I drive past the great marsh. Black clouds gather on the horizon like a large clenched fist.

The wind is getting stronger, making leaves stick to my jacket and grazing my face and hair like thousands of fingers.

Utterslev Marsh.

I get out and walk along the path down to the water. From the lake a raw smell of swamp hits me. In the direction of the invisible city center I see the tower of Our Saviour's Church, its erect, verdigris-green corkscrew against the sky. From here I can see her apartment with its view of the first of the marshes. Her building is large and white, with a wide, black mansard roof. The windows of the top-floor apartments look like the eyes of a flirtatious glass doll.

I smoke a cigarette, then drive to the paper.

In my office I go over the list I got from Stella. I'm groping in the dark. She's given me a selection of the names she came up with when she expanded the search to include Jacob Roth Pascal—all the names with a direct connection to Los Angeles.

There's a French-Canadian biochemist connected to a Danish project who makes scale drawings of proteins for a biology information center. Stella has appended a few articles about amino acids—in which he's cited in footnotes—that she found in a cross-check. There are two English reporters, one for *The Guardian,* the other a motor-sports reporter for a monthly magazine. There's an engineer with technical expertise in software promotion, a biologist affiliated with the Australian Immunology Research Department at Commonwealth Serum Laboratories, an astrologist, a pilot, a designer. I keep reading, but I'm having trouble concentrating.

Then I pull out everything in the electronic archive on pornography and scan through miles of articles. Most of them I discard; a few I save, print out, and read.

I get a cup of coffee from the machine. Return, sit for a while, and look around my office. Cut-outs on the walls, photos, telephone numbers. I no longer feel any connection to any of it. Once I was proud of my profession. I wanted to help people. Carry the weight of the world on my shoulders. But, like all other great responsibilities, the weight forced me to my knees. The young Molberg was a temperamental firebrand fighting for the weak; defender of the downtrodden, the ostracized, the poor. The young apolitical Molberg would never accept any doctrine, never proselytize for any belief or ideology; to him all ideologies were lies, because they canceled out other ideologies which were just as reasonable. He never wanted to be tied down to a position, and never made a choice, because one choice excluded other equally worthy choices. He wanted to stay free, flexible, receptive to all points of view. Or perhaps he just wouldn't commit himself; it all depends on your perspective.

I remember when the world ahead of me was full of possibilities. Then came the end of childhood, school, a job which could have been almost anything, because at the time that wasn't what mattered. Before me lay a new world with new faces, new ways of looking at things, new experiences, and a new identity which in weak moments seemed to compensate for what had been lost. Every human being betrays himself. We start dying the minute we're born, but only a few of us have the privilege of not knowing that.

Reception calls up when Lindvig arrives. I hurry downstairs. We're on our way.

He's driving, so I tip my seat and lean back.

"What did you find out?" he says.

"Greater Los Angeles is the center of the American porno industry. In Denmark we buy and rent porno films to the tune of more than six hundred million crowns a year. The amount goes up to more than a billion if you include the black market."

"I read a survey that said that only one person out of ten rents a movie with ordinary sex," he says.

"Did they interview anybody but you?"

He smiles.

"Just be glad I have to concentrate on driving," he says.

We head out of the city, crawling through heavy traffic on Freden's Bridge. Then we come to a total halt.

"Where exactly are we going?" I ask.

He looks at me.

"Remember that question. Then think about it again in a few years. Before long, cars will have digital road maps, and instead of sitting there being obnoxious, you might be sitting with a 'bodytop,' or whatever it's going to be called, digging around in your paper's database to do the homework you should have done earlier. You didn't find anything useful?"

"No," I say. The traffic inches forward. "It's really sick."

"According to your numbers, there are a lot of sick people," he says.

"The future," I say. "I meant the future."

He looks at me, surprised.

"Why's that?"

"Who's going to be checking the computers?"

"Other computers."

"And what are *we* going to be doing?"

He smiles. "Goofing off."

Lindvig's world is still a fantasy, but there's no doubt that it's coming—with all its marvelous improvements and unavoidable breakdowns. I gave up when everyone else did. When I think about all the pieces I wrote that were never printed because the editorial board felt that the fear of technology was over! When I think about the gruel of information that sloshes around in the system! Of course there are safeguards. But everyone knows that no system is any more secure than its weakest link. There are all sorts of ways to screw up. Even the most highly trained accountants and number crunchers can make mistakes when they think they're on the track of something in a company's annual report, or some of the entries, or a suddenly altered accounting practice; and the most skilled doctors can overlook a fatal piece of pathology.

"All you want to see is the negative," Lindvig says. "Right over there." He points to the buildings of the National Hospital. "They have scanners, electronic surveillance of cardiac patients. One day chaos theory may be able to discover why the HIV virus breaks down the body's immune system. The next thing may be artificial life."

"As opposed to what? Real life?"

"I give up," he says.

The wind pulls at the car. At the outer reaches of Nørrebro, Lindvig turns into a parking lot paved with cobblestones. A relatively new commercial property, the building has a hipped roof and is situated in a sunny slot between tall, faded buildings.

"Here," he says. "And remember that you don't even know how to spell the word *reporter*. Let me have the photograph."

There's a man standing behind the counter as we enter. The only people I dislike more than three-button-suit types and tattooed apes are tattooed apes in three-button suits. That's what he looks like. He's neat and grubby at the same time. His body is too muscular for his clothes, his clothes too classy for his body. He has fierce eyes and a small, scruffy mustache.

"Who's that?" he says, motioning to me.

"He's okay, " says Lindvig. "He's with me."

"I don't like you bringing people."

"This is an exception. We're looking for a guy."

"One for each of you?" he says, laughing at his own joke.

The mood eases as we laugh with him politely.

In a room where all the shelves are filled with porno films, Lindvig puts the photograph on the counter.

"This is the guy," he says.

The salesman bends over the photograph. In the corner of the room, a small color screen shows a movie in which a redheaded woman is heaving her crotch up and down over an erect penis. The sound has been turned off. The door to the left of the salesman opens, and a man in a smock appears. He looks like a druggist. I'm surprised the place isn't larger until, through the open door, I see a storeroom packed with films.

The young, pudgy man in the smock puts a pile of papers and a few cassettes on the counter.

"Hoff, do you know this guy?" asks the salesman. The man in the smock picks up the photo and studies it.

"I think we have a few films he's in."

"French? American?"

"No, Danish. He's Danish," he says.

"Are you sure?"

"You can never be sure when it comes to sex, you know."

The man in the smock is concentrating. "I don't remember his name, but if you come back tomorrow, I'll know."

"How about Jack or Jacob Pascal? Jack Roth Pascal?"

"No, no. He's Danish. His name is something Danish."

"Does he do magazines, too?"

"I don't know. I only see films, but the actors usually do. What do you want him for? Does he owe you money?"

Lindvig points to the monitor. "Is that a Bang and Olsen?"

"No, it's the new Sony," the salesman says.

"Not a bad picture."

"Which part?" says the salesman.

He laughs. We laugh. The man in the smock laughs. I turn to the man in the smock again. "How many films do you have with him?"

"If he's the one I'm thinking of, at least a couple."

"We'd like to have all you've got."

The salesman looks at me quizzically. "We *do* have other stuff."

"No thanks, this is my man."

"Whatever. To each his own."

The man in the smock goes toward the backroom door.

"Why don't you call tomorrow? I'll have something then."

"Anything else I can interest you in?" asks the salesman.

"No thanks," says Lindvig.

The salesman turns the photo on the counter and smiles.

"Who's the babe?"

Lindvig pulls at me. "Come on, we're leaving."

I pick up the photograph and leave a few bills.

"Who's Jack Roth Pascal?" asks the salesman.

"We'll know that tomorrow," I say.

Then we leave.

Lindvig drives me back to the paper.

"What are you going to do when you find him?"

"I don't know. Reduce him to some form of artificial life."

The bouquet is large and white and looks unreal. Like feathers plucked off a swan.

Sometimes you can feel these things instinctively. Before I go out there, I know something's wrong.

Just before I reach the airport, I almost stop and turn back. But I go on, even though our agreement was to meet later.

In the arrival hall I find some of her colleagues. They say she's already left.

"What time did you land?" I ask.

"We had a tailwind," one of the girls answers quickly.

At that moment I realize that Natasha's been lying to me. That is, I think she has. And yet I can't quite believe it. It seems unreasonable, unlikely that she'd really lie. There are periods in your life when the thought of other people lying to you is completely intolerable.

I drive back through the city. On the other side of Amager Island I notice the Mazda in the back mirror. It follows right behind me all the way across Town Hall Square, past the Lake Pavilion, and down Borup's Allé. Only after Borup's Allé, just before the hill, does it turn off. I drive on slowly, watching for the car in the mirrors. But it's gone.

Slowly dusk lowers over the marshes, and a pale blue fog sails like colored air across the water. Underneath purple clouds on the horizon, a hazy yellow sun quivers coolly. On the farthest lake, tiny silver boats ripple the surface of the water.

My hands shake slightly as I drive down her street. I park the car across from the building and turn off the motor and the lights. In the dusk I light a cigarette. There's light in her apartment, but the curtains are drawn.

The lover.

When the curtains are pulled open, I see Natasha in the window with a stranger. The embrace doesn't look anything like a good-bye hug.

I roll down the window. Throw away the flowers. Then I leave.

I fill the glass with ice. After four or five shots everything falls back into place. I get a loving, inexplicable urge to embrace everything. Buzzing, I float through golden whiskey spirals.

When she arrives, I look like a madman. Dragging myself to the door as she rings the bell, I slide down the doorjamb, and she has to catch me before I hit the floor. She drags me into the living room, where she sits stroking my hair. I half-doze. Then she gets up and goes to the bathroom. I struggle to my feet.

As I stand in the bay window, I hear her behind me. Like a black shadow she slides in front of me, the pill container in her hand. There's something dangerous about her that's different from Monique. She undulates on slim, black, silky legs.

"What's this?" she asks, holding my Thorazine.

"Just something for dizziness."

"Don't you think it's time you told me about yourself?"

"You know as much about me as I know about you."

"Oh, you're impossible." She takes a step away from me.

I turn around angrily.

"*I'm* impossible?" I walk up to her. "What about this? Bangkok?" I say, holding her arm tightly.

"What do you mean?"

"It's real, Natasha. It's not from Bangkok."

She tears herself loose. "So what? What's it to you whether it's real or not?"

"I just think it's strange."

"And what about you? Sitting around drooling over the letters of a dead girl."

Suddenly she's furious.

"You know about it?" I say.

"Of course I know."

"How?"

"Who gives a shit? Everyone knows. Why are you saving all that junk?"

"Junk?"

She doesn't want to be weighed and measured and compared to a girl from my past. But doesn't she know that we'd never have met if I hadn't been making comparisons? Does she really care at all?

"You're sick," I say.

She gets up angrily, walks away, then returns and throws another container of pills at me.

"Am *I* the one who's sick?"

The lid comes off the container, and the white pills spread all over the floor like hail.

Silence.

Then, as I watch, she gets down and starts picking them up, putting them back one by one into the container. Am I violating her? Am I merely acting out the whole thing through her in order to change the ending? Or is it to prevent what happened from happening? Or is it to watch everything happen again?

"Say something, Martin."

I look at her.

"Why didn't you tell me you knew?"

"You didn't tell me anything, Martin. What was I supposed to say? What does one say?"

I don't answer.

She sits.

"Why don't you tell me about her?"

"You know already."

"Not everything."

"What do you want to know?"

"Everything."

I stand up. "I don't know, it's all so messy. They still don't know who did it, and they think it's me. But I was here. I was at home that evening."

"She meant a lot to you, Martin, didn't she?"

I don't know what to say. I'm confused. Yes, she meant a lot to me. But what exactly? In the apartment I can still hear her giggles, and sometimes I see her in the street in the faces of other girls: a neck, a profile. As they turn around, I suck in my breath when I see it isn't her. Monique's parents identified her. Perhaps I should have done it—should have touched her cold body, looked at her last, closed, purple face. Just so that I could have believed it. Maybe I'm like a woman who can't grasp what happened until she holds her stillborn baby at her breast. Only then can you believe. Only then can you take it in.

"Have you spoken to anyone about it?"

"Not really," I say.

"It helps, Martin."

"Who says?"

"What do you mean? You're not the first person who ever lost someone he loved. Not everyone just sits around feeling sorry for themselves."

"That's enough!"

I grab her face. Start squeezing.

"What is it you want? Tell me what you want!"

"Let go of me, Martin."

"Do you want to know how many times he came? Is that what you want to know, Natasha? Do you want to know what really hurts? I'll tell you. They found her one evening in a basement. The crazy thing is that we didn't even know anyone who lived there. What do you think she was doing there? Tell me! What exactly was she doing there?"

I shake her face and slap away her hand when she tries to twist herself free.

Tears are welling up in her eyes. She's afraid, shaking.

"Let go, Martin. You're hurting me."

"Answer me!"

"Maybe someone forced her to go down there."

"There was no sign of that. What was she doing there?"

"Meeting someone?"

"Do you know what hurts? That they think I did it. Because that's the only thing that makes any sense to them. And there's something else, one small detail. The body doesn't always obey the heart. That must be the explanation."

"What do you mean?"

"Monique had sex before she died."

"Sex? You call that sex? Wasn't she raped?"

"No. Because, as the police expressed it, there was 'no sign of a struggle.' She probably knew her murderer."

"Maybe she was terrified!"

"Terrified? With a cunt so full of juices that you can't even call the small cuts rape? She was sopping wet, Natasha. So it had to have been me. The only problem is that it wasn't. So who was it?"

Then I shout:

"Why the fuck was she so wet?"

She's crying. Tears are running out of her eyes. I loosen my grip.

"Don't hit me, Martin."

I walk over to the couch and sit down. She's sniffling and wiping her eyes with angular little hands. Then she pulls herself together.

"But what about semen?" she says in a small, brave voice. "They must have found some semen."

"Not if he used a condom," I say weakly. "And who the hell ever heard of a rapist using a condom?"

"God, I'm sorry."

"So am I."

Natasha is silent and red-eyed. The bags under her eyes are yellow and puffy; they look like mosquito bites.

I walk over and sit down beside her, put my arm around her.

"I'm sorry. I don't know what came over me."

I kiss her cheek. It's salty.

"I'm a little scared of you right now, Martin."

I hold her tightly.

"You don't have to be."

"Maybe I should go home?"

I shake my head.

Exhausted, she gets up, walks into the bedroom, undresses. A little later she comes back and stands in the doorway.

"Are you coming?"

"No, I'm going to stay here for a bit."

She walks toward me. Then stops halfway.

"What's wrong?"

I look at her.

"Who was at your apartment today?"

"Are you spying on me, too?"

"I happened to be passing by. I was going to visit you, but I left when I saw you with someone."

"I don't think I need to be accountable to you."

"Of course not."

"A friend. An old friend. Jesus, you're paranoid."

She leaves. A moment later the light in the bedroom goes out. I lie down on the couch.

Later that night I get up and walk over to the bay window again. I stare over at the black windowpane, thinking that perhaps I ought to tell Natasha about Monique, the photograph, the bank account, and about Dr. Phillip and Jack Roth Pascal. But I don't. It's just a feeling. I know that she knows something, but I don't know what. I want to know what she knows. I have to find out what she knows.

Teeth chattering, I sit in the dark living room until Natasha calls for me from the bedroom. I tell her I'm coming.

Suddenly she's standing in the doorway.

"You're acting so strange," she says.

"I'm sick."

She sits next to me, putting her arm around my shoulder. I feel a vague sense of discomfort, nausea in her presence. Typical of a personality disorder, Dr. Philip would say.

"Maybe we ought to take it a little slower?" she says.

"Maybe."

She says she's going to go to her mother's summer house. If she does, will she think about me? I don't know. Will she send me a postcard? What will she write? Will she write the way Monique did, or write about the weather? Or is someone up there waiting for her? In that case, will she write to me about him? Probably. Women always let you know about things like that. Will she merely make fleeting references to him or say outright that she's found a lover? Yet another one? I don't know. I don't know anything about her.

"I think I need to be alone for a while," she says.

I get up and walk over to the window. It's ajar; a cool breeze hits my face.

"With whom?"

She sighs, gets up, and walks over to put her arms around me. She puts her face against my back.

I turn around.

We stand like that for a while, holding each other.

"You're shaking," she says.

"So are you."

"I'm cold."

"So am I."

The rain is drawing streaks down the windowpane. From a nearby backyard a cat wails like a woman who's been neglected too long. An erotic lament in a backyard underneath the roofs. Before long the high school students will be graduating. Not so many years ago, I used my student cap as a protective covering with a girl so as not to stain her mattress. It was at one of the last graduation parties. Our principal's name printed inside the cap was almost dissolved, and the cap felt oddly limp when I put it on to go home that morning.

I don't know what I expected of the world at the time. Or of the future. I don't remember. Now I don't expect anything at all.

I stand in the bay window a while longer while Natasha sleeps.

Just before the bang I see something. At least I think I do. Underneath the trees on the street something moves; a quick fluttering. Then, for a moment, there's nothing. Then the flash of light, the pressure, and rain of glass when the black windowpane and the apartment across the street explode.

Chapter Thirteen

A few minutes later, the street is filled with fire engines, police, and ambulances. Swirling blue lights sweep the facades where people at windows are craning their necks to see what's going on. Children awakened by the noise are crying, and some women are crying, too; a few elderly people on collapsible stretchers, in shock, are being carried off. A police car blocks the cross street to traffic. People in nightclothes and coats stand in the glass- and debris-covered street, chatting with the police. In their white jackets and red helmets, a few firemen direct operations with walkie-talkies while others insert another hose into the broken window after the first one springs a leak; water gushes into the street from the leaking hose. Seen from above, the hoses all look like strands of spaghetti snaking around the cars.

Most of the apartment has been destroyed. Later that night, when they finally get the fire under control, what's left of the place looks oddly like an outdoor terrace. We have to keep our windows shut to keep out the smoke. The woman across the street is standing by her window looking at us. I see one of the photographers from my newspaper talking into his cellular phone. Most likely to the crime desk. I call the paper, get his number, and call him. As I stand in the window, I watch him take the phone out of his breast pocket.

"Molberg?" he says. "How the hell did you hear about it?"

"I live here. Look up."

He turns around, looks up, and smiles when he sees me.

"What's the word?" I say.

"Sounds like suicide. A young guy. They say he turned on the oven and all three gas burners in the stove."

"Don't you think there's something strange about it? I was watching when it happened."

"Did you tell the police?"

"I didn't see anything."

"They'll probably question you anyway."

"But don't you think it's strange?"

"What are you getting at?" he says.

"I should have seen something—a flash of light, maybe. Something."

"Not necessarily. If the gas was on long enough, it wouldn't have taken much. It could have been his refrigerator that sparked it. That actually happens. Did you know him?"

"No. I didn't even know anyone lived in that apartment. I never saw him come or go. I never even saw a light. Actually, I never saw any sign of life at all."

"Well, you're not going to now," he says.

The entrance of the building is filling with people.

"Looks like something's happening, Molberg. I'm gone."

I watch him run toward the ambulance, where people are carrying what may be the charred remains of a body. Flashes of light in the dark.

I give up trying to sleep. Even when it begins to get light, the street, flooded with water from the hoses, still buzzes with activity. Police officers chat calmly with curious onlookers from the surrounding apartments.

"I'm taking a bath," says Natasha, walking past me quickly. Soon I hear water running in the tub.

I'm trying to imagine what it feels like to be blown up. To survive an explosion but then burn to death. To try to escape while everything—including you—is melting. At eight to nine hundred degrees Celsius everything melts. Fire reaches upward. One's only chance is to lie on the floor as far away from the center as possible. But even then it's tricky. Once I had to cover a fire. When the rescue people brought out a young woman, everyone thought she'd miraculously survived. Until they turned her over very carefully: her entire back was black, and her skin had cracked open like dry earth. She had third-degree burns all over her back. Later, she died on a respirator.

When she returns from her bath wrapped in a big white towel, Natasha is silent. She goes to the bedroom to dress.

"I'm going into town. Do you want a ride?" I say.

"No, I'll take a cab."

I pack my things. She doesn't ask any questions. She doesn't suggest anything. She says nothing.

"Don't forget to lock up," I say.

"Is there anything here worth stealing?" she says.

Later that morning, I call Hoff.

"I found him," he says. "I've got three films. You can have them for a thousand."

"What's his name?"

"Just a moment. Nikolai Martin," he says.

"Nikolai Martin? Is that his real name?"

"Probably not."

"I need his real name."

"That'll cost extra. Another two thousand."

"That's okay."

"Drop by in a couple of hours. I'll have it for you by then."

I scan the papers for stories about the explosion; generally they confirm the earlier reports of the young man's suicide. An older woman suffered a concussion when a heavy object fell from a shelf above her bed and hit her on the head. Probably it's the old lady. I look for more information in the internal database, but there isn't anything else.

From my window I see Stella on the street and call down to Reception to stop her. Then I reserve a table at the Three Towers and go down to meet her.

"My treat," I say, hooking my arm through hers.

"Are you writing a dissertation?" she says while we're drinking our coffee. "I have some more names for you."

"That's what I wanted to tell you. You don't have to search anymore. I've found him."

"You have? Was it one of the ones I gave you?"

"I don't know yet. But I'll know soon."

"Are you sure this is considered work? You know I'm not supposed to do anything on the side."

"Of course it's work. You know that."

She looks at her watch. "I've got to go now, Martin." She gets up. "Thanks for lunch." She smiles and puts her jacket over her shoulders.

"I do have one more job for you," I say.

"Who is it?"

"Natasha Noiret."

She frowns.

"Who's that?"

"I don't know," I say.

He's alone in the shop wearing his smock when I arrive. I place the money on the counter.

"So what's his name?"

"Well, I'm going to hit you for the two thousand anyway, but actually his real name *is* Nikolai Martin."

He puts the films on the counter.

"Do you have a phone book?" I ask.

"You don't have to look him up. I put his name, number, and address into one of the cassettes. Do you want a bag?"

"Does that cost extra?"

He smiles. "No, it's on the house. Here you are."

When I'm on my way out, he says:

"We're not going to have any trouble, are we?"

"I don't think so."

"Who are you, anyway? We know Lindvig, so we know you're not a cop. Are you a reporter?"

"Do I look like one?"

"Pale, suspicious, unpredictable. Yes, as a matter of fact, you do."

I open the door.

"Don't worry, I won't write about it. And if I change my mind, I'll call you."

"That's what I mean. Unpredictable," he says.

Slowly I drive along the street. The apartment is in what used to be called the Black Square, in a small side street off one of the lakes. I park the car and sit for a while. He's supposed to live on the second floor, but there's no sign of life in the windows. After a while I open the door and walk over to the entrance, scanning the nameplates. The address is right; the name is right.

I go back to my car and wait. Smoke a cigarette. Nothing happens. I wait.

After a couple of hours I leave.

⁂

"Murderer!" shouts the old lady. I run over toward her, but she shuts the door before I get there.

"Sick bastard! Murderer!" she says, and hits the inside of the window in the door with her cane. The bandage on her head looks like a turban. Then she makes her way laboriously up the stairs, leaning on her cane.

The janitor is right behind me.

"Don't worry about her," he says. "She's a little nuts."

He's about to leave.

"How well did you know that young guy?" I say.

"Me? I didn't know him. No one did. I spoke to him once when he took over the lease. That was last winter."

"What was his name?"

"Tom Kubjec."

"Do you know what he did for a living?"

"No idea. I asked him when he moved in, but I didn't get much of an answer. He studied something. I think he was involved in politics of some kind. He was very secretive. We never saw him, and most of the time I don't even think he was living in the apartment."

"I don't think so either. Actually I don't think I ever saw him."

"He always used the back stairs. The backyard has an entrance around the corner. That's why you don't see anything on this side. He was very shy, maybe because of his face."

"What about it?"

"He was disfigured. Had some ugly scars on one side. Maybe that was why. It couldn't have been easy to live with. The police think it was suicide."

"That's what they say."

He shakes his head. "They'll probably figure it out when they find the other one."

"What other one?"

"The one who visited him that evening."

"How do you know someone visited him?"

He looks at me, frightened. "Why are you asking so many questions?"

"Who visited him?"

"I didn't see anything," he says, and starts to walk away.

"Take it easy," I say, trying to catch his arm, but he tears himself loose and quickly disappears past the cordons by the tarps at the gate.

He looks back over his shoulder.

"I know who you are," he says. "I know what you want. I don't know anything. I didn't see anything."

Then he disappears through the gate. It doesn't matter. I know what you saw. I know what you know.

In vain we keep searching for the etiology of my suffering. Something must have triggered the disease. But it's hard. And who really knows why anything is the way it is? Maybe the truly wise ones are the ignorant, and the wise are wise only because of the dilemma of the ignorant—which is that they're too ignorant to realize that ignorance is true wisdom. And so on. If there's a shadow of truth in Freud's teachings, then by definition I'm the only one who can't see my past clearly.

I see Monique in front of me. The photograph. I turn it over and over in my head. Night after night, filled with thoughts which consume me. Sometimes I wake up soaked with sweat—some nights, several times. Shaking and terrified. There are some nights when I don't even dare move when I wake up because I sense that I'm not alone in the room. Why such fear? What is it I see when I close my eyes?

Dr. Phillip worries about these paranoid incidents.

"Perhaps we ought to try some Prozac," he says.

Poor doctor. The psychological definitions won't behave the way he wants them to; the facts won't fit the theory.

Crossing his arms, he takes his usual seat in the chair. His elbow rests in one hand; his lips are pursed; his forefinger taps; his eyes are thoughtful.

He says: "At least the apartment explosion would seem to rule out your conspiracy theory, don't you think?"

"I'm sure someone's been watching me."

"You don't seriously think that the police gained anything by blowing themselves up? Besides, the papers say it was suicide."

"I'm a reporter, Dr. Phillip."

"What do you mean?"

"Information doesn't come out of thin air—it comes from somewhere."

"So it's been coming from the police, who now are trying to cover their own tracks? Is that what you're trying to say?"

I shrug. "I don't know what I'm trying to say."

I'm sitting in the chair opposite him. He'd prefer me to lie on the couch.

"Only to help it flow more freely," he says.

"I'm jumpy," I say.

I get up, walk to the window, rest my hands on the sill, and look out.

"Did you know, Molberg, that psychology isn't completely unfamiliar with fantasies that actually materialize?"

"What do you mean?" I say, turning to face him.

"All this talk of being watched. Being followed. Someone spying on you. A black windowpane. Someone looking at you. Could it just be guilt? A feeling of guilt?"

"That apartment *exploded*," I say. "And two months ago the woman who lived opposite it was murdered. Coincidence? Paranoid fantasy? Don't you think that it's just a *little* peculiar?"

He looks at me.

"Jung. Do you ever read Jung?"

I look at him, tired.

"Sometimes, " I say. "When I can't fall asleep."

Guilt? Is it really that banal? Was Monique Milazar actually an angel I rejected ruthlessly, and was I somehow responsible for her death? Is that what's been plaguing me all day long and haunting my dreams so that I have to create imaginary external threats to justify myself? Did I drive her away?

I can still feel her presence, even though she's no longer here. I can still remember her, even remember the scent of her wet hair and skin after a morning bath.

Was it all nothing but pheromones? Nothing but the heavy fumes of desire?

She taught me to love, and I lost her forever. She taught me to love—or did she teach me to lose? Or is it the same thing?

Once they were all queens, princesses of our dreams. Where did those images come from? And when did everything fall apart? Was it when it became clear that the dreams could never be realized, or the first time the foundations on which they were built were abandoned? Was it when the first compromises were made, the first apologies spoken?

We're on a relentless hunt for the traumas of the past. The kernel that released the unconscious intrapsychic conflict, as Dr. Phillip says in his somewhat abstruse manner. When I talk about walking in the forest and along the lakes, he smells a longing to return to the womb.

"Wasn't that what Freud never understood?"

"What do you mean?" he asks.

I shake my head.

"How do I know if you're even asking the right questions?"

"I've been through analysis myself," he says.

"And I'm a journalist."

"That's different," he says. "The questions are different."

"But how do I know if I'm being asked the right questions? What if I don't have the answers to the questions I'm never asked? What if *you* don't?"

"Now you're theorizing again."

"Am I?" I say. "How do I know that the pain I'm feeling is so wrong? How do I know that *pain* is wrong? How do I know that *I'm* wrong? And how do I know that I'm not *supposed* to be wrong?"

"It all sounds very peculiar," he says.

"I'm not an empiricist."

He looks at me triumphantly. "And how do you know that?"

I walk back to my chair.

"Why is it always all about my mother?" I say.

"Well, I don't think you've had much of a relationship with your father," he says.

"Maybe he's the problem."

We're not making any progress. To an outsider it may look as though he's treating me, but he isn't really. It's all bluff.

Dr. Phillip was trained during a period when the profession enthusiastically embraced electroshock treatments. For a few seconds the symptoms simmer with pain, then they are gone. In the roar of the moment, something that isn't actually sick might also be lost, but that is taken into account beforehand.

When you're a child, you think the world is full of absolutes. Large, serene concepts. That's why abstract art frightens children. When you grow up, you realize that the world is full of abstract art.

Dr. Phillip doesn't give an inch. But neither do I. I refuse to be subjected to his terminology. So we find ourselves in a constant stalemate. He calls me crazy, I call him crazy. But it's only when I say it that it sounds crazy.

There he sits behind his words. Behind them are more words, and behind those even more endless rows of meaningless words. When they meet any resistance, they close up around themselves. A closed system impossible to penetrate. Because of its meaninglessness. An impenetrable mass, comparable to the euphemisms of politicians. You finally give in. Because you don't understand them. And because you're unable to formulate anything that has meaning.

"It's perfectly natural that you feel anger toward me," he says, as though we're on the brink of a classic therapeutic breakthrough. "This is very common."

"I don't follow you," I say.

He leans across the table.

"You'll just have to have faith that I can help you."

"I'm an atheist," I say.

"That's enough!" He bangs his fist on the table, then catches himself and quickly begins, with false calm, to rub the spot. Our cooperative venture has completely collapsed.

"You know what they did to me at the hospital, don't you?"

"They were only trying to help you, Mr. Molberg."

"Help me? Every time I picked my nose, they gave me electroshock."

"It was only to help you. You weren't yourself, Mr. Molberg." I feel tired.

"Then send me back," I say. "Give me more electroshock."

He stops his tapping and looks at me with annoyance.

"We prefer to call it el-stimuli, Mr. Molberg."

The rain draws nervous streaks down the windowpane. On lonely treetops across the street, crows beat their black wings. Distantly.

Pushing one of the videotapes into the machine, I grab one of Natasha's duty-free bottles. The special vintage is wasted on me. I fill the glass with ice and pour the whiskey like beer, comforted by how little she paid for it. Like a mystical drug, the expensive liquid makes me into the person I really am. Or would like to be. Without melancholy or anxiety. Now I have the coordination of a ballet dancer and the eloquence of a book. I've had goals in my time—clearly defined ones that could only be reached, oddly enough, via detours. When I drink, I'm as focused as a shark.

I have this constant dream of simplicity. To be simple. To have simple dreams, simple sorrows, simple worries. It'll never happen. If it could, I wouldn't have to dream such dreams.

On the screen a black girl with swollen red lips is licking a deformed, swelling lump of flesh that finally becomes a hard rocket with a veil of saliva and slime at the root. Holding her tightly by her unmanageably frizzy hair, the man makes her body heave backward while he drives in and out of her, her buttocks quivering. Finally a close-up of the vagina's little pink hole, shutting with a foolish, gaping expression, and then her black, arched back, a small pool of moisture, and little transparent beads on her ass.

Did he say to Monique: "Are you afraid of me?"

And did she say: "Well, I don't feel completely safe."

"I'm sorry about that."

"It was a compliment."

Was that what they said? Was that how it happened? In my dream I strike out at a face, and it breaks. There are some images we simply will not see.

The tape rolls silently as the black girl gets buggered by another man and a woman lies underneath licking her. Nikolai Martin's out of the picture. I get up and open one of the bay windows. Maybe I doze a few minutes, resting on the sill, and I don't see it right away; but then suddenly something across the street moves. I realize she's been there the whole time. The woman in the house across the street.

As always there's only the dim light from the TV. It's as if I've had membranes covering my eyes, but now it slowly takes form. Suddenly I see the outlines of her body. She's slid off the couch onto the floor. Her body forms a taut arch; completely naked, her crotch pushes forward. Both her hands are working. But is it a fruit, a vegetable, or an actual dildo she's using to find the inner rhythm?

Other nights, I've seen oddly blurry, indistinct faces on her

TV screen, but now I realize that I've been all wrong. What I see now is a crotch filling up the entire frame. I see lacquered, pointy fingernails pulling back layers of skin and folds. I see the shiny, damp, peach-colored interior pressing down onto what can only be the head of a penis.

Her face, which has been fixed on the screen, now turns toward me with a strangely helpless expression, twisted with painful abandon. I don't know if she really sees me, but it seems to me that her rhythm grows more intense as she looks in my direction. She is looking at me who is looking at her looking at the screen. Perhaps we're a kind of mutation, the first of a generation that has become fixated on looking, and whose greatest realization is also its curse: that life can only be looked at.

It's like witnessing a murder without any opportunity to intervene. As if shot from behind, she throws her body forward, shakes in a spasm, then collapses on the floor, limply, like liquid.

I feel so tender toward her. I want to go over and stroke her hair. But I also feel nauseous. Maybe it's the whiskey.

I call her. Slowly, she gets up and puts on a bathrobe, then goes to the window and picks up the receiver.

She looks over at me.

"What do you want?"

"Just to chat."

She holds the whole telephone in her arms. "I like it when you look," she says, changing the picture on the screen with her toes.

"I like to look," I say.

"It's pretty sick, you know."

I laugh. She walks back to the window, then smiles across the street.

"Did you jerk off?"

"No," I say.

"Why not?"

"I don't know."

"Didn't you think it was sexy?"

"Oh yes."

"Are you afraid of Mrs. Palsborg?"

"Who's Mrs. Palsborg?"

"Her." She points next door. "The woman in number eighteen. I'd have committed suicide too if she was my neighbor."

"She calls me ugly names," I say.

"Why? Are you spying on her, too?"

"No."

"Then that's the problem."

"Can't anyone else see what you're doing?" I ask.

"Sure, lots of people. But you're the only one who looks."

She yawns and stretches.

"I'm so tired now."

"Then go to sleep. I didn't want anything."

She looks over at me. "Then why did you call?"

"Actually I just wanted to thank you. I've never had a chance to thank you."

"For what?"

"For that night. For the fact that you were home, and that you saw me."

"What are you talking about?"

"My alibi. Didn't they talk to you?"

"Yes, but I didn't see anything. I wasn't home that night."

Chapter Fourteen

I sleep until late afternoon. My hair is greasy, my pants so dirty they could bite. The salty foam from a couple of Alka Seltzers leaves a fishy taste in my mouth.

The police confirm what the first investigations indicated, and what was obvious anyway: the explosion destroyed the gable from the third floor to the roof, and the rubble fell to the street in piles almost six feet high. The police dogs found no more bodies in the rubble. In the kitchen, all three gas valves had been turned on, and the first assumption of the rescue workers and the doctor—that the deceased had been dead before the explosion—turned out to be correct. In a word, suicide.

"Is there any more to write about the case?" the policeman on duty asks when I call up.

"That's what I'm trying to find out," I say. "What do you know about possible causes?"

"Well, either a spark or a flame ignited the gas. We'll probably never know for sure."

"There must be clues."

"Not many. The firemen hosed the place down pretty thoroughly."

"What about witnesses?"

"Nobody saw or heard anything." He laughs. "Aside from the explosion, of course."

"The man's name was Tom Kubjec. Do you know what he did for a living?"

"Worked for a company called DiaData. Some kind of service agency. Commercials, things like that. We've talked to some of his colleagues. Nothing earth-shattering. He was pretty private."

"Did he have a visitor that night?"

"Not that I know of. We probably would have found another body."

"I heard that it might have been his refrigerator that sparked it."

"That's a possibility. It takes almost nothing."

"But no one knew anything about a visitor that night?"

"No."

"Suppose someone rang the intercom. Would that have been enough to spark it?"

"Theoretically, yes. It's been heard of before. But it really depends on how long the gas was on. And, like I said, no one rang the intercom."

"No one that you've spoken to."

"That's right."

"Thanks for your help."

Someone comes to visit. He enters by the back stairs, no one sees him. He hits the man over the head, turns on the oven and burners, and puts the man headfirst in the oven. Then he quietly leaves. By the back stairs? Probably. When the gas has been on for a while, he passes the front door and rings the intercom. Boom!

Maybe the janitor heard something. Or saw something. Either he heard the steps on the back stairs, or he saw the visitor in the backyard. Or he heard the ringing just at the time of—or a fraction of a second before—the explosion. Maybe the police already talked to him, but he said nothing. Or maybe he did say something in the middle of the confusion, but no one made the right connection. That's what must have happened. The janitor knew that Kubjec was expecting a visitor that night, or that someone had been there. Just before the explosion, I saw something in the dark. I saw something that moved. I saw the murderer. And in the seconds after the explosion, with flames gushing out of the apartment and rubble flying, he disappeared, unobserved, in the shadow of the tree in front of the building.

I consider calling Klinker. But I don't. From now on he won't believe anything I say anyway.

The telephone rings. I don't answer it. The answering machine kicks in. Lindvig.

"Pick up! I know you're there!"

I get a knife from a drawer in the kitchen, sharpen the blade on a whetstone, and weigh the handle in my hand. I wipe off the metal dust with a dish towel. The telephone rings again. Lindvig.

"You're not doing anything stupid, are you?" he says on the machine. "If you're thinking about doing anything stupid, call me. You can buy people for that sort of thing . . . Forget it, I was just kidding. Call me."

I put the knife in my inside jacket pocket, then call. No answer. I get into my car.

I park in the same place as last time. In the back mirror I can keep an eye on the cars coming and going, as well as on the entrance door.

Only when you're the one waiting in a parked car do you think you look suspicious. Passersby may look at you but won't pay attention. Not if they go by only once.

At the end of the afternoon a yellow Mercedes rolls into the street from behind. It parks right in front of the door. Even in profile I know it's him. Before I have time to think, I'm out of the car and across the street, knife in hand. It all happens so quickly that I bump into the hood as I round the car. My foot hits a rock and I have to steady myself against the hood. I drop the knife. The sound makes him turn, but by then I'm right behind him.

The attack is so sudden and so violent that he has no time to defend himself. I strike his chin cleanly; it's as if he's been given a signal to drop. He falls, flailing his arms just before he hits the sidewalk. My hesitation gives him a chance to collect himself and get back on his feet. Fear and confusion fill his face; he has no idea what's happening. I'm on him again, but this time his arms shoot out and his elbow hits my eye. We stumble and fall, and when I land on top of him, he knees me in the crotch. I feel like I'm about to throw up; I can't move. His hands grip my neck and start squeezing.

"Crazy bastard!" he says, pressing until my throat is about to burst. Slowly, feeling returns to my legs.

We both get back on our feet, but now I'm being dragged. He doesn't let go. My strength surprises him; I don't know where it comes from. It must be a chemical reaction, the gathering and releasing of energy just before a catastrophe. I don't know how it happens. I'm on top of him, hitting his face hard twice; the third time, he goes down. My feet strike his teeth, and something cracks both in his mouth and in my hand. He falls sideways, groping for me with his hands, but I've struck him

cleanly and he tumbles forward, stumbling clumsily, half scram-
bling, half crawling to get back on his feet. I throw myself on
top of him and with all my might hit him in the back of his head.
The first blow only glances off his head and ear, but the second is
direct to his head; it's as if all life functions in his body stop. He
falls forward and lies immobile. His arm jerks a few times as if
short-circuited. I grab hold of his hair and twist him around.
Then I grip his collar and gather it firmly in my left hand.

"Nikolai," I say. "Or is it Jack?"

Blood draws tiny streaks on his teeth as he whispers, "What
the fuck are you doing?"

"A new name calls for a new identity," I say. "I'll give you a
new face."

Before I know it, I have a rock in my hand. I lift it.

Then there's a sound of screeching brakes, and shouts.

They've practically thrown the car sideways on the street.
Both officers hold loaded guns.

"Drop it," they shout. "Just drop it."

Slowly I let my arm fall.

They approach.

"Get off. Get off him," they shout at me.

I get up and retreat a few steps. The officers come closer. Siren
howling, another patrol car arrives from around the corner. People are leaning out of their windows.

"What's going on here?" one officer says, fumbling for his
handcuffs. The other still has his gun pointed at me.

Nikolai Martin gets to his feet, slowly wiping the blood from
his dripping nose. His cheeks are smeared with blood and his
nose is crooked; it looks like it's broken.

"He attacked me!" he says. "He jumped me!"

The officer with the handcuffs approaches me.

I'm licking the back of my hand to cool my frayed knuckles.

"Turn around," he says. "Arms behind you." I stretch my arms backward, and the handcuffs shut around my wrists. Then I see the knife lying under the car, but they don't see it. The officers grab my jacket and lead me to the patrol car, while the officers from the other car come over and put handcuffs on Nikolai Martin.

"What the hell have *I* done?" he says.

They lead each of us to a patrol car.

"What did you do to her in Los Angeles?" I shout.

"What are you babbling about? I've never *been* to Los Angeles."

A hand pushes him into the patrol car, and the officers lead me away.

"Asshole!" he shouts. The door shuts, and they drive off.

"You've got to explain yourself, Mr. Molberg. One just doesn't go up to people and attack them."

Dr. Phillip is tapping.

"Actually all that anger could be a positive sign. But it can go too far." He looks at me thoughtfully.

Then I notice Max Klinker talking to one of the detectives. He's picking though his dry, thin hair. Some people go bald in a curiously withered way, as though their lives have been so dissolute that their hair breaks off in pale, dried-up stalks. That's what's happening to Klinker, although I doubt that his life has been dissolute.

"What's Klinker doing here?" I say.

"I thought he might be needed. I'll talk to him," says Dr. Phillip.

He goes to Klinker and the detectives. I can hear him explaining about the treatment, that it's progressing, and about unavoidable setbacks and traumas.

Klinker comes over.

"So, Molberg, have you had time to calm down a little?"

I nod.

"You know, you just can't go around beating up people. I suppose you know that!"

I nod.

"Is your head clear?"

"Completely."

He scrutinizes me.

"We don't have to add anything to the report. Is there anything you'd like to say?"

I shake my head.

"And you're sure you don't know him? You just suddenly went berserk?"

"I don't know him."

"You're not holding anything back, are you, Molberg?"

"Yes, but I'll try to control it," I say.

He looks at me, annoyed.

"All right," he says. "I don't think there's anything else. We've talked to Mr. Martin and explained your somewhat . . . special situation. He's still pretty confused and upset. I don't know yet if anyone will press charges, but I don't think so. However, you're looking at a civil suit, damages, things like that. But I suppose that's getting off easy."

"Can I go now?" I say.

"Yes. That's about it." He turns to leave.

"What was he saying about Los Angeles?" I ask.

He turns.

"About Los Angeles?"

"Why does he say he's never been to Los Angeles?"

"Maybe he never *has* been to Los Angeles. What does Los Angeles have to do with all this?"

I look at him. "Everything."

Aimlessly I ride through the northwestern sections of the city. "I've never been to Los Angeles." How can he say that when I know he has?

I drive across the city. The traffic exiting from the highway is murderous, so I take the winding residential roads along the marshes, passing Natasha's apartment, and at a telephone booth just before Brønshøj Square I pull up and park. I call Marianne. She's not at home. Of course the man may have been lying, but he sounded honest. He sounded convincing.

Sitting in the car, I study a road map, smoke a cigarette, then set my course for the industrial section of the city.

I have trouble finding it. The low factories and warehouses all look alike, and the signs range from the obtrusive to the self-effacingly anonymous.

The buildings of DiaData are farthest away, in a row of new commercial structures. The complex consists of three boxy gray buildings with a few black glazed windowpanes. I check the numbers of the neighboring buildings to make sure I have the right address. There are no signs at all: they could be making plastic here, machine parts—anything at all.

The only distinctive feature about the buildings is the security: most of the other properties are fenced in, but a solid wall runs around the entire complex; broken bottles line the top of the wall like a jagged edge. A few cameras have been placed discreetly at the entrance, where two guards sit in glass cages. Everything's effectively blocked by an electronic gate.

I park provocatively close to the entrance by the side of the road, letting one of the guards have a full view of the car. Then I light a cigarette and wait.

It only takes ten minutes for him to come out of his cage. Calmly he walks up to the car, like a traffic cop, and knocks on the window. I roll it down.

"Are you having problems?" he says.

"Who isn't? What's yours?"

"You can't stand here."

"What are you guarding in there? The Crown Jewels?"

"You can't stand here."

I turn the key and start up the engine. Then I roll forward a bit and stop right in front of the entrance. I roll up the window, and now he comes up to me. I see the other guard leave his booth and head toward me, too.

The first guard hits the roof of the car hard.

I let down the window again.

"What do you think you're doing, asshole?"

"We've got you on film, buddy," he says.

"Make sure you watch it with a consenting adult," I say, stepping on the gas.

Back home, in front of the TV, I sit down and spool through the films with Nikolai Martin. Lindvig tells me they use some kind of sugar mixture for sperm when the male stars can't perform, so even in this kind of movie, the female stars have to worry about their weight.

In Los Angeles the day has just started. I call the hotel and ask for Louis, listening to all the clicking on the line while I speak to Reception. When they put me on hold, Vivaldi's *Four Seasons* floats through the receiver. Perfection. Monique brought the CD back once from one of her trips. Suddenly I have a strong urge to listen to the whole thing.

The music is interrupted.

"Louis here."

"This is Martin Molberg. I don't know if you remember me. I stayed at the hotel a little while ago."

"Of course, Mr. Molberg. How are you?"

"Louis, it's important. I've got to know if she was there."

For a moment he's silent.

"She wasn't, sir."

"Is anyone there? Is it hard to talk now?"

"Yes, sir. That's right."

"Are you absolutely sure, Louis?"

"Hold on, sir." He puts his hand over the receiver, but I can still hear him. "Yes, Miss, can I help you?"

Then he's back again.

"I hope this is important," he says. "I'm risking my job doing this."

"It's important, Louis. Very."

He doesn't say anything.

"I thought we were friends, Louis."

"We *were*. But they're talking about you. There are people here talking about you."

"People? What people? Who?"

He covers the receiver with his hand again. "Yes, Miss. Just over there by the concierge."

He removes his hand again, speaking quietly.

"She wasn't here. I've been in the computer, and she wasn't here. Not under that name. Couldn't it have been taken at a different time?"

"No. People? What people?"

"My pleasure, sir. Good-bye."

The connection is broken.

She was there but she wasn't. Nikolai Martin was there but he wasn't. Of course he was there. He must have been there. But the sentence keeps buzzing through my mind: "I've never even been to Los Angeles." How can he say that when I know he was? I know he's been there. I can see it.

On my television screen, images flicker. It's one of the videos. A nurse is taking the temperature of an overexcited female patient. There's a doctor standing behind the door, and before long he joins in the fun. Enter Nikolai Martin, playing the shocked husband discovering his sick wife's antics in the hospital bed.

The telephone rings. It's Stella.

"Martin, I think I've got her," she says.

On the screen Nikolai Martin has also joined in. When you spool back and forth, it's easy to see that this is what he planned from the beginning. He throws the nurse onto the bed. The wife's illness isn't nearly as serious as the IV and cardiogram machines indicate. Now the doctor's examining her throat. He throws up his hands: nothing wrong. So he stuffs the contents of his pants in there instead. Cut to Nikolai Martin humping the nurse. I freeze the frame.

"Just a moment, Stella. Can I call you right back?"

"Sure."

"Where are you?"

"At the paper."

"I'll call in a moment."

I rewind slowly. Then pause the frame. Then slowly forward. Then back a tiny bit. There. I take out the photograph and compare. That's it. That's exactly how he looks in the photo.

I go to the kitchen to get a glass. Pour a large whiskey, and swallow a Thorazine.

I call Marianne again. No one home.

On the screen Nikolai Martin is frozen in position behind the nurse's ass. He's missing a tooth now, and Molberg will have to pay for it. "I've never even been to Los Angeles." How can he say that? The set switches from the video to the regular TV channel. Twelve little frames, flickering like live creatures. I switch back to the video, then spool back and forth a bit. Freeze the frame again. *He's* right: in the video he's in the exact position of the photograph. But *she's* wrong. Her face is buried in the hospital bed. In the photo Monique is looking up, facing the camera directly. And he's behind her, in exactly that position.

It *must* have been taken in March. Monique got her new hairdo in March. I take out my calendar and leaf through it. Slowly, with great deliberation, I run my fingers over the days. It must have been then. Monique had her hair cut in the last week of March. Two days before her death she dyed it. So the photograph must have been taken within a period of three or four days. There aren't any other possibilities.

I get up and start searching for *The Four Seasons* on the shelf of CDs. I want to hear loud music. A swirl of violins and sparklingly clear flutes. But I can't find it. I kick the shelf, and a pile of CDs falls out, their fragile covers coming apart and ice crystal-like cracks appearing at the corners. This bothers me even more, and I kick the pile angrily.

I try Marianne again. Finally she's there.

"Molberg? What do you want?"

"There's something important. Monique had her hair cut in March while she was living with you. At the end of March. During that time she also went to Los Angeles. Exactly when did she go?"

"Just a moment, Molberg. I just walked in the door. I'm sorry, what were you saying?"

"Do you remember how long Monique lived with you?"

"I'd say almost a month. But you know that yourself."

"I just want to be absolutely sure. When in March did she go to Los Angeles?"

"Los Angeles?"

"Yes, it had to have been the last week."

"She didn't go to Los Angeles that week. She didn't go there in March at all."

"Are you sure?"

"Absolutely."

For a while I sit with the receiver in my hand, looking at the screen.

"Thanks, Marianne."

Finally I begin to see the light. Finally. I've been so stupid. A photograph can't document anything, yet it can be *used* to document just about anything. I read that somewhere.

They can do that kind of thing today. Of course they can.

I call the paper and get Stella on the line.

"I'm sorry it took a while."

"No problem. Let me pull her out," she says, clicking the keys.

"Where did you find her?"

"She's not mentioned anywhere, but I found her in the insider file." She taps the keys. "Here she is. I hope you're not falling in love, Martin."

"Why not?" I say, but before she says it, I've already guessed. It can lodge in your consciousness like a small, disturbing flicker. A reservation. It might be something a person says or the way she behaves. As a reporter you train yourself to pick up that kind of thing. Sometimes more than you really want. With Natasha it was the few minutes in her apartment. The lavishness of her home, which had no relation to the level of her income.

"And we're quite sure?" I say.

"There are several reports about her. She worked out of the SAS Royal Hotel a few times, and there are the names of a few customers. Politicians."

"So she's a whore. Definitely a whore."

"A prostitute, Martin. Definitely a prostitute."

"What about Jack Roth Pascal?" I ask.

"I thought you'd finished with him. Didn't you ever find him?"

"I was wrong. He wasn't the right one."

She starts tapping keys again.

"Let me see if I still have the list. Do you know more now? Who do you want?"

"I think I do. There was an engineer, someone who worked with computers."

"I've got him. Jacob Roth Pascal. You already have all I had on him. It wasn't much. But I can try again on the Internet and a couple of BBSs. When do you need it by?"

"As soon as possible. Preferably tonight."

"Is your modem open?"

"Yes."

"Okay, then I'll send it if I find anything."

"Thanks for your help, Stella."

"No problem, as long as it's for a story."

"Does it mention what her price is?"

"You ought to be able to get a discount, Martin."

"It's strange. In a way there's something innocent about her."

"That's the way some men want it."

"What kind of men?"

"What do you think an answer to that question would cost you?"

"I don't know. You tell me."

"Good-bye, Martin."

I go in and turn on the printer. Then I bring the telephone directory into the living room and call Lindvig. He's working.

"Where have you been?" he says.

"I've been talking to Nikolai Martin."

"Talking to?"

"It's not him. I don't think he's the one."

"Why not?"

"He says he's never been to Los Angeles."

"But that's a lie."

"Maybe not."

"What do you mean?"

"Do you remember the photograph?"

"Sort of."

"Monique has short blond hair in the picture. She had that done the last week of March."

"So?"

"I've had it all wrong. Monique wasn't in Los Angeles during that time."

Silence at the other end of the line.

"It's been doctored," I say. "The photograph was doctored. There's no other explanation."

I can hear the printer start up, so I go in and skim the first few pages while it's typing them out. Stella was lucky. Jacob Roth Pascal, American engineer and software producer; lives in the US; has lectured on cryptography in a number of countries, according to one source who answered Stella's query. Was associated once with TDI, says another. I put a question mark by TDI. No details. Nothing about where he lives now. It's not much, but it's better than nothing.

I put down the paper and let the printer keep printing, then go back and eject the video from the machine. When the printer finishes, I collect the white sheets about Jack Roth Pascal and put them with the videotape.

In the living room I light a cigarette. She's listed in the phone book as Mona Noiret. There are two listings with that last name. I pull on a jacket while I punch in the number. After a couple of rings someone picks up. I tie my shoes, the receiver wedged between my head and shoulder.

"Hello."

"The summer house. It belongs to Natasha, doesn't it?"

"Hello, who's this?"

"It's not yours at all, is it?"

"Who am I talking to?"

I hang up. I know the answer. The only thing that makes her human is the fact that she even has a mother.

Chapter Fifteen

Lindvig studies the photograph carefully. He shakes his head.

"If it's a fake, it's incredibly well done," he says.

"It's a fake. It has to be a fake. The question is only, how was it done?"

He shrugs. "Well, that's hard to say. They had something to start from, of course. They could have used someone else's body, but that seems unlikely. It is her body, isn't it?"

"Yes, I know Monique's body."

"Take a look at this," he says, pulling down a few windows on the computer—or the workstation, as he insists on calling it. As far as I'm concerned, it looks the spitting image of what I consider to be a computer: screen, keyboard, mouse.

He opens a screen.

"In principle, you can do anything on today's computers," he says, clicking the mouse. A simple line drawing appears on the screen. "This is the first image in a typical animation sequence."

The picture is of a room—white lines on a black background. Furniture and objects are suggested with simple lines: coffeepot, table, lamp, mirror; odds and ends. The scene is drawn from above. It doesn't especially impress me, compared to the doctored photograph lying next to it.

"Just wait," he says. "It's orthographic, meaning without perspective. You've got to go through the whole progression. Take a look."

He clicks to the next frame.

"Now we've zoomed down, and we're looking through the eye of a camera lens into the room. You see the objects the way they'd look in an ordinary room. It's still a line drawing and transparent, but we've added depth cueing. The polygons are drawn toward the vanishing point. This creates a sense of depth, just as in reality."

He moves to the next frame. Color has now been added to the lines, but they're still matchstick-like. Then color is added to the areas, but in flat planes, so that the picture looks like the first stage of a watercolor.

He clicks again.

"Here we've added shading. It's connected to individual planes, defined by the free-standing polygons. This is a simple way to achieve perspective."

The picture is beginning to look like something. More color; color nuances and shadings on lamps, coffeepots, ashtrays. But it still looks artificial, something like a cubist drawing with clear, dense color surfaces.

"Now comes one of the most important elements: Gouraud's algorithm. Smoothing, we call it. Or discontinuity."

It's beginning to look lifelike. Shadows have become deep and intense, and highlights have been added to the objects. Still, the picture doesn't look quite real.

"That's because," he says, clicking to the next frame, "only now do we take the highlights into consideration. Here's the same picture, but done with a different algorithm. Phong shading, it's called. It's much more realistic because it examines the effect of light in each pixel in the object, but for that reason it's also much more computer-heavy. In this picture you can tell that more sources of light have been added. There's light in the lamp and on the table."

The last picture he clicks to reveals the total manipulation. From lines we've arrived at a picture almost indistinguishable from a photograph. The mirror on the wall reflects the objects on the table, which in turn reflect the shiny, lacquered surface of the table; the light is perfect. Like magic, via menu formulae, single lines have been transformed into something that fools the eye completely.

"This is what's called photorealism," he says, clicking the images off.

Then he picks up the photograph and scrutinizes it.

"In principle it could have been made the same way, although it looks extremely lifelike. Normally you'd start with an image, a photograph, several photographs, perhaps. You'd scan them into the graphics program and then start developing it."

"And then you'd superimpose it onto the background?"

"The background doesn't have to be genuine," he says.

"But how can that be? I know the room. The wallpaper. The mirror. I've stayed there. It's the Four Seasons."

"Not necessarily."

He opens another window, then goes into a few menus, clicking on a window in which a sphere of dark-brown, wood-tone colors appears, complete with shading and highlights.

"Procedural textures. Formula-based imitations of basic structures such as wood, clouds, marble. They can be mixed and colored totally according to one's wish. There are thousands in a software package like this, and each can be manipulated so that the variations are endless. You can create exactly the kind of background you want."

I eject the video that's already in the machine and replace it with the one I brought along—the one with Nikolai Martin.

"Take a look at this." I fast-forward a bit, and Nikolai Martin appears in the hospital sequence, virile and tanned.

"What do you want me to look for?" Lindvig says. Then he slowly leans forward and scrutinizes the pictures with immense concentration. "It's *him*," he says. "What should I be looking for? It really *is* him."

I shake my head.

"It's Nikolai Martin, but I doubt he's ever even heard of Monique."

"You've lost me," says Lindvig.

"Wait a second. Let me freeze the frame." I forward slowly, then pause the picture.

"There," I say.

"What?"

"Look at the photograph, then at the screen. The same picture."

He looks at the photograph. Looks at the screen. Looks again at the photograph.

"Exactly the same," he says. "It's actually exactly the same."

"Except for Monique. She's missing. She's been added."

He brings the photo all the way up to his eyes.

"You can't tell. You can't tell at all."

For a moment he seems delighted that he can't detect the manipulation.

"I think it's disturbing," I say.

Lindvig stares at it, enthralled. Either he's impressed by the falsification, or he's exulting in the childish delight of having been fooled.

"In a way, it's incredible how badly we see," he says. "It's perfectly awful." He gets up and launches into a monologue about the weakness of our vision. Do I realize that our vision is stereoscopic, and that it reacts only to light within wavelengths of 3900 to 7700 angstroms? That we're capable of differentiating between 1,200 nuances of gray but don't see colors very well? And do I realize that the three-dimensionality of the world isn't something we can actually see but something we learn from infancy?

I shake my head. All this is vaguely familiar, but my head is spinning. As a reporter without any one specialty, you tend to skip from one thing to another. You dig, you read, you call up, and, in the course of a few days, you've become an expert on a fragment of reality. Very often only a fraction of the information you've unearthed turns out to be of use, and very soon most of it is forgotten. It's on a par with cramming for an exam: you grind through the material for a particular occasion. Only now and then do bits and pieces of knowledge and data stick. All I can remember is that no one read the heavy, overly researched articles we wrote on Japanese protectionism and the emerging revolution in wide-band video. Since we were writing about TV anyway, the higher-ups at the paper thought we'd do better to attack famous people.

I get up.

"We have to get someone to examine the photograph," I say. "I have some contacts, but I doubt they know much about image manipulation. Do you know anyone who's into this sort of thing?"

He's still studying the photograph. Slowly he wakes up. And nods.

"How much are you willing to pay?"

"Anything. But it's got to be done as fast as possible. Preferably right now."

"Do you realize what time it is? Go home; I'll call you if I find someone. It won't be till tomorrow at the earliest."

I go over to his bookcase and let my finger slide along the shelves.

"Do you have anything on image manipulation?" I say.

He thinks for a minute. He searches the shelves and picks out a few things. A bit of nighttime reading for Martin Molberg, who isn't likely to be kept spellbound by the technical jargon. He leafs through a couple of computer books, some journals, and some newspaper clippings. Then makes a pile of it all and hands it to me.

"Here. Read. How much can it cost?" he says.

"It doesn't matter. The only problems I don't have right now are financial."

As I drive home, it strikes me how unreal everything feels. Before it also felt unreal; but now it feels so real that it feels unreal.

Man looks in front of him; it's built into his physiognomy. Eyes close together, turned forward and set in cavities on the front of the cranium. We have no natural enemies. We have no other weaknesses than the fact that in more ways than one we can't look backward. At the expense of our other senses, we've made ourselves slaves of our vision. We are therefore easy to manipulate.

Lindvig calls just as I walk in the door. He's found an instructor from Symbion Copenhagen Research Center: Stig Plaun, expert in digital image manipulation.

"We'll go out to the Polytechnic University in Lyngby. They've got some equipment we need. Tomorrow night."

"What time?"

"We'll discuss that tomorrow. He wants to be absolutely sure we'll be alone."

He pauses for a minute, then says: "You're thinking about something. What?"

"The photograph. What I don't understand is why it's so important. Why is someone so interested in getting hold of it? If Nikolai Martin didn't commit the murder, who did?"

"But maybe he did," says Lindvig. "Did you ever consider that the photograph might be genuine? Or at least the situation. Couldn't it have been the background that was copied in?"

"I've looked through the tapes, and she's not there. He is. And I've established a connection between Monique and the hotel. It's too obvious. And then there's Nikolai Martin. If there had been one detail that was off. But there isn't. He's been lifted right out of the film."

"A photograph can't document anything . . ."

"But it can be used to document just about anything. Precisely," I say.

"I'll pick you up tomorrow night."

"Stig Plaun," I say. "Who is he?"

"The best," says Lindvig.

Nighttime. The city dozes with black eyes. I sit in my work-room and read and chain-smoke till dawn. Smoke fills the room like a thick fog as I wake up with my head on the desk in the middle of piles of papers and magazines. I open the windows to the backyard and lean out to get some fresh air. The cornice, dotted with white and gray pigeon droppings, looks like a Picasso palette. From the other side of the yard the pigeons' throaty cooing echoes back.

I have a headache and a taste of dead mouse in my mouth. I carry the brimming ashtray to the kitchen and add a couple of Alka Seltzers to a glass of water. The magic tablets dissolve like whirling snow in the glass; with a sudden snap, they remove the pain and give me new life.

I sit in front of the monitor and wait for *Publicom* to open. Then I punch in.

DiaData is Danish-owned, it tells me; according to the com-pany books, the primary stockholder is the large media con-glomerate Tele Trois. This, plus a few other minor details, is all I can get from their records.

I'm no accountant, so I can easily be duped as I sit leafing through data, trying to formulate an overview. The company seems solid and sound. But it's so easy to be fooled. There's the glossy paper with the balance sheets, the auditor's endorsement and annual report; there are the profit-and-loss statements, the profits divided into categories of either product or function; the external expenses, personal expenses, write-offs. There are plant assets, negotiable assets, backup securities; on the debit side, the net capital, long- and short-term debt. Somewhere behind this hierarchy of entries and headings is the actual status of the "pa-tient," but that may prove extremely difficult to ferret out.

As usual, I make a note of all names of people in managerial positions and such, but none of them seems familiar. One lawyer's name rings a slight bell, but that's all. Tom Kubjec isn't mentioned; apparently he's further down in the hierarchy.

Aside from the direct line to my paper, *Publicom*—online database of the Association for Businesses and Corporations—is the only database I'm hooked up to. I've used it several times, mostly when we have to demonstrate some name overlap, make a connection, or find a name to help us with a story. Along with the accounts, the accountants' remarks are subdued and cautiously optimistic. They're hopeful about a series of "new initiatives." But of course they don't specify what the new initiatives are. That's the only interesting thing I find.

I'm no genius at navigating inside the databases. Stella tells me that there are people who've become rich simply by having the ability to move around in them. At one point, thanks to Stella and the database *Rapid,* our paper's political staff was the first to publish the new directives from the EC Commission in Brussels. The commission holds a daily press conference, and a few hours later all of it is accessible on *Rapid.* The only thing the system required was that the reporters be multilingual, because the news was available still only in the original languages. A few days later, the transcripts of the press conferences were available to the public in the three major languages. In newspaper terms, a few days' head start isn't considered outdistancing—it's downright outclassing. Stella knows a lot of tricks.

Everything's become so fast. Information sweeps, friendships, disclosures, scandals. News comes at us in such volume that, when you put it all together, it becomes oddly unimportant; it cancels itself out. Everything's speeded up. Only sex has to go slower and slower, even though we are in a rush with everything else.

Its buildings like large, dark, children's blocks, the city glides by in the darkness. There are very few cars in the streets. The bluish evening light faintly illuminates the low houses that lie slumbering like a dark body. This desolate section of the city has always reminded me of an endless dormitory town—a taste of the suburbs of the future. We pull up in front of one building.

"There he is."

A tall, bespectacled man wearing a turtleneck sweater and a large coat stands by the entrance. Stig Plaun.

Lindvig shuts off the engine and pulls the hand brake. Then he turns to face me.

"He hates ignoramuses, so pretend you're just a tiny bit familiar with names like Cray 1 and Silicon Graphics."

"Which are?"

"Supercomputers. Plaun just bought a Cray 1 at an auction in London. A Cray 1! In the middle seventies it was the fastest in the world. Today it's museum material—six feet high and weighing ten tons. Don't ask either me or Stig Plaun how he expects to have it transported to Denmark; I don't think he's figured that out yet. Back in the seventies the Cray 1 cost nineteen million dollars."

"What did he pay?"

"Ten thousand, one hundred and one dollars, and one cent."

"A binary number," I say.

"You *have* been reading," says Lindvig.

"All night long. What does he want it for?"

"Collector's item. But it was also a pretty good buy: the machine contains sixty thousand dollars worth of gold."

"So why doesn't he sell it?"

"It's a sacred trophy. He wants to have it in his house as some sort of monument to the past."

I know right away that I won't like Plaun. I don't believe in progress, for the simple reason that progress isn't progress anymore. Progress is a leech, a parasite whose greatest accomplishment is to be able to allay, at a later date, all the catastrophes it creates. One could say that this is the argument for both its birth and its death—it ends up a wash. I'm aware that the view of progress depends entirely on the eye that sees it, and the way it sees it. Meanwhile the future, with its own peculiar life cycle, continually makes promises which only it can honor—in the future. And the worst thing of all is that we can't see any of this because our fascination with progress has become a fascination with progress alone.

As we walk toward Plaun, he's not smiling; he looks like someone who is cold and bored and has suddenly realized that he's in the wrong place.

He shakes Lindvig's hand. "It must be very important."

"It is," says Lindvig. "This is Martin Molberg." We greet each other.

"Are you the one who's paying?" he says.

I nod.

"May I take a look at it?"

I show him the picture.

He brings it up to his face and studies it closely. Then he holds it at arm's length and brings it to his face again.

"What's the story?" he says.

He's like a doctor. The subject doesn't interest him. He's already searching for defective dots. He looks right past the subject. He is looking for the weakness in the picture itself. His task is simple. He has to find the flaw, and that's what he's looking for. That's the only thing he's interested in.

"There's something wrong with it," I say.

"I see," he says.

"It's been manipulated."

He smiles condescendingly.

"Well, on the surface there's nothing that immediately suggests that," he says.

"Could you say for sure that it *hasn't* been worked on?"

"No, but to be completely sure, I'll need to spend some time with it."

"I can't let it out of my sight. We'll stay."

"It may be a waste of money."

"I *know* that picture's been through a computer."

"How do you know?"

"I just do."

He looks at his watch.

"If it wasn't for the mirror, you wouldn't get me to do it. But okay, let's take a look. Come on."

We walk quickly down the long hallways in the building, which is deserted except for the cleaning staff. He unlocks the glass doors that separate the various departments.

Then he stops in front of a locked door, searching for another set of keys.

"What about the mirror?" I say.

"It's there," he says.

In my view, people like Stig Plaun represent the future. He's a digital disciple, a mathematical messiah. People like him have not only embraced the new technology, they have entered it; they have disappeared into a universe in which the planets are artificial and God speaks in codes.

The computer on the table looks like any ordinary computer. But it isn't. It is, he explains, a Silicon Graphics RISC-based workstation. "A so-called supercomputer. Just a bit more powerful than the one you work at," he says, smiling. "George Lucas's corporation, ILM, owns eighty of them. Only NASA has more. Makes you think, doesn't it?"

Lindvig listens with interest. I try looking awed, but I can't. I'm not impressed. I don't grasp it fully. He can tell.

"What do you know about Silicon Graphics?"

I look at Lindvig. Then I shake my head.

"Not much."

"Cray?"

"Cray is good," I say.

He frowns disapprovingly.

"Cray and Silicon Graphics make supercomputers. If the photograph's been manipulated, it was almost certainly done on one of those. Supercomputers are used a lot in the animation industry—for television ads, things like that."

In the research we did for TV articles, I recall that we touched on this. Large parts of the film industry have been working for a long time on the electronic layering of pictures. It simplifies the editing.

I remember some figures, some calculations that said that if cars had developed as fast as computers in the past twenty years, they'd be able to reach a speed of 500,000 miles an hour. For television the story's simpler. During the fifty years of its existence, almost nothing has happened. When you consider the importance of images in people's lives, that's incredible. We remember in images; we create images of people we know and people we don't. They're imaginary—but they're images. We dream in images, fantasize in images, and, for thousands of years, we've expressed ourselves in images. Which doesn't change the fact that the resolution of ordinary television sets is pathetic.

This is the multinationals' argument for new technology. The real reason, of course, is that the market is saturated. But this is their problem: the human eye has adjusted to coarse picture resolution and manages to fill out the flickering image with color and form itself, creating the illusion.

Plaun places the photograph on a glass plate in a scanner next to the Silicon Graphics computer at the back of the room. He presses a few buttons: a ghostly light blinks under the lid of the scanner.

"You always have to be alert when you run across a picture with glass or metal, mirrors, smooth surfaces, things like that. Pictures are illusions. Just as with magic, you're lured into looking in one direction while the actual illusion is taking place in another. If reflections and shading have been placed correctly, they'll fool the eye. They'll create a sense of space and authenticity. That's why computer graphic artists like to use mirrors in their manipulations. And that's why we're on our guard."

He waits while the machine is scanning. Then he starts tapping the keys and pulling down various windows.

"First we'll try pumping it up. We ought to be able to pump it up six to seven hundred times so we can take a look at the pixels."

He zooms in, then out again, then in and farther in. He aims at her body. Gets closer and closer. The outlines of her body disappear; close to the breast, skin becomes points, life becomes pixels.

"How do you know this is a forgery?"

"The room is in the Four Seasons Hotel in Los Angeles. The hairdo in the picture, she had it done during the last week of March. At that time she definitely wasn't in Los Angeles."

"Hmm," he says. He zooms out from the body again and moves up to her hair. Then zooms in again. Very close.

"But she'd been to Los Angeles before."

"Many times."

"To this hotel?"

"Probably."

"So in theory the picture might have been taken of her there?"

"I suppose so."

"But you don't think so, right?"

I hesitate.

"No."

He looks at me insistently.

"You don't think that you think so, or you don't think so?"

"I don't think so."

"Okay," he says. "We'll go for the hair first. What was her hair like before?"

"Long."

"Then they'll have removed something," he says. He moves out into the area around her face. Enlarges sections, then zooms out again. He moves up close to her hair again.

"What do you see?" I say.

"I was hoping we might find something there. Bump-mapping. You often use it to create texture in an object. Mostly for granulated surfaces, but also for other things. Including hair. Normally, if an object has been manipulated, you can see its edges clearly. This doesn't look that way. And they'd have had to re-create the area of the picture which used to be filled with long hair. It would have been detectable. But it isn't."

"I thought I read that one can't actually see the manipulations anymore."

I can tell that that irritates him. He looks directly at the screen.

"I can."

He works with incredible speed. It's hard to follow what he's doing. "I'll try something else," he says. The machine is doing something. He pushes away from the table a little and folds his arms on his chest.

"What now?"

"We count pixels," he says. "It's incredible how unclear this picture is."

When the machine stops, he turns toward it again and clicks to a menu.

"Peculiar," he says.

"What?"

"Well, it's not an ordinary photograph."

"Why not?"

"What do you know about photographs?" he says.

It sounds slightly patronizing. I smile.

"The basics. That a picture is worth a thousand words."

He looks at me. "I thought reporters were supposed to know a little about everything."

"Who told you that?"

"A reporter."

"Then you shouldn't believe it."

He looks at me, annoyed. Behind Plaun's back, Lindvig smiles.

"Well, you may know that a photograph consists of lots of tiny dots. The degree of the resolution is measured in DPIs, dots per square inch. Points or pixels, as we call them."

I nod. He's speaking exasperatingly slowly.

"A normal paper photograph consists of twenty million pixels. A slide, of about a hundred million pixels. But this is different: here there are only a few million."

"Which means?"

"That something's missing."

"What?"

"The other twenty-four pictures."

I look at Lindvig and Lindvig looks at me. Neither of us quite gets where Plaun is heading.

"Film. We're talking video. Digital video film," he says. "What we're looking at here is a single frame from a film that's been lifted out and printed as a paper photograph."

Chapter Sixteen

Maybe Stig Plaun actually sees colors as the numbers they are. To me that's hard. The problem with the unreal room is that its unreality is so difficult to hold on to. So hard to grasp. She's right there! It *is* Monique! If I could follow the sequence of pictures, she'd move, come alive. I remember the time an old man collapsed in front of my eyes in the middle of a Copenhagen street. I did what I could. What I ought to. To be kind, the ambulance people told me that he died on arrival at the hospital, but I know that he died in my hands. I have the same feeling now. Although it seems I can do something, there's really nothing I can do.

Monique received a package while she stayed at Marianne's, a package the size of a book or a videotape. I'm trying to re-create the course of events, to imagine how she would have reacted, how she might have been thinking. The problem is that I'm no longer sure how she did think. I'm fumbling around in unreal space.

"Since we know that they fiddled with some of the things in the photograph, how do we know that the hair is the only thing they touched?"

He looks at me.

"We don't," he says.

"I thought you said that you'd be able to tell?"

"Normally I would. But not here. In computer-treated images you've got to hit some very precise numbers. You change colors and expression in the picture by using certain numbers. It sounds simple, but it isn't. Every color or raster has its own angle on the paper. If you're sloppy, small explosions can occur in the picture when you layer one color on top of another. Interference. In order to control the raster angles, you often have to go as far as five or six decimal places. It's pretty complicated work, even if the finished product may look effortless and convincing. It's all in the details. Most amateurs slip up as soon as they have to put in the light and shadow—the completely banal things that the naked eye can see. Shadows that fall wrong, things like that. But that's not the case here. This photograph's clean, flawless."

Finally it dawns on me what's wrong. Finally! A simple detail. A banality. I stare at the monitor for a long time to be sure.

"Zoom in on her hand for a minute," I say.

With jerking movements he focuses on her arm, her hand. The computer processes. A murky image appears.

"Can you make it sharper?" I ask.

"A little sharper is possible."

He pulls down menus, clicking the mouse. Then the picture is drawn again, moved, contracting around itself, becoming sharper.

"The ring. The ring is missing."

I imagine I see pity in Lindvig's eyes, and I wonder: Is this a suddenly awakened sensitivity in him? He says reluctantly:

"It's possible that she took it off."

"Monique never took it off. She thought it was bad luck to put it down somewhere. It was our engagement ring."

Lindvig looks at me with exasperation. It becomes him to feel pain.

"If there was a film . . . *that* kind of film . . . If she was in one of those films, she might have taken off her ring."

I smile, nodding at him.

"Yes, but like everyone else who wears a ring most of the time, she would have had a pale, narrow line on her finger. It would be very noticeable because she was always tanned. But there," I say, pointing at the screen, "you don't see it."

They don't say anything. Lindvig seems to be looking for an explanation which he can't find. Plaun pulls down menus and zooms into sections of the picture, but he's not really focused on it. I can tell that he's not thinking about the picture now but wondering what this is all about.

"So you know the woman?"

I nod.

"And she's not the type to be in that kind of movie?"

"No."

"And you can't recall any photograph of her they might have used as a starting point?"

I shake my head.

"I don't have any that come close to this sort of thing," I say.

He sits staring at the screen. Enlarging single elements, zooming in, panning. He vacuums the image but finds nothing.

"Let's just say that she has something on them," I say. "I don't know what, something. They fight back, send her compromising photos. The film. She alters her appearance. They alter the appearance of the image in the film. It all happens within a few days."

Plaun stares thoughtfully ahead of him.

"It would mean a lot of work, but it is possible. They would have to change the area around her face. But where did they get the first photograph of her?"

I shrug, then remember the videotape and take it out.

"I don't know where they got her from, but I know where they got him. Can we use the VCR over there? This is a regular VHS tape."

He nods. I insert the tape, take a few steps back with the remote, and turn it on. Plaun watches me curiously. I fast-forward to the hospital scene, then stop. Forward a bit more, then freeze the image. Forward slowly, then freeze again.

"There," I say, stopping the tape.

I get up and stretch. Plaun looks at the screen in disbelief.

I pick up the photograph and study it. Not even when you know is it possible to tell. They're there, but not there. It's too much to fathom. The problem with unreality is that it's so hard to grasp, to take in. I try visualizing their movements, but I can't.

"So when it comes to her, we don't know for sure that they had anything to start from?" asks Plaun.

I shake my head.

"Not for sure."

"And I'm assuming that there's a particular reason that we don't just ask her?"

I nod. "She's dead."

Lindvig stares vacantly. It's as though he's still looking for a plausible explanation. An objection. For him, this just doesn't compute.

Plaun has stood up; he's pacing. I don't know if the fact of

Monique's death has registered, but it doesn't seem to interest him particularly—except as a piece of information that makes the photomanipulation that much more interesting.

"So the photograph was used as blackmail, you say?"

"That's only a guess," I say.

"We can't rule out that there may be a film with her in it," says Lindvig.

I look at him.

"No, but if there is, why would they change her hand?"

I try to imagine a course of events. There is a film. We know there is. That was the package that was sent to Monique when she was staying at Marianne's. Monique hid the package. Or threw it out. In any case, she reacted. She changed her hairstyle. She must have known how desperate her response was; all they needed to do was change her image. She cut her hair short. That was at the end of March. A few days later she changed her hair again. This time she dyed it, because in the meantime she'd received the photo we're looking at, in which they'd changed her long hair to short. I know I'm fumbling, I know there are huge holes. But it's the only thing that makes any sense. Since they had nothing to start from, they made a mistake when they made her hand; they forgot the ring. No one says a word. But we're all thinking the same thing: they created her on a computer.

"What you're saying is that they animated her from scratch?" says Lindvig.

"I don't know. I'm guessing," I say.

Lindvig's doubtful, but his doubt is beginning to annoy me, because his skepticism has nothing to do with critical objectivity. Instead, it comes from his wish to defend the technology—from his refusal to see what it's being used for.

"What I'm saying is that they changed her hair, manipulated it so well that we can't even tell. And then, God knows why, they gave her a hand that wasn't hers. If they can do that, why couldn't they falsify the whole thing?"

Lindvig shakes his head.

"Because it isn't possible. We're not talking about a photograph, we're talking about film. Do you realize how many bits of information they'd need? Do you realize how many bits of information even one second of that film would require?"

I don't know what else to say. I can't even see most of my assumptions. I can't take my suspicions and show them to others. All of it exists only as a picture in my head.

I look at Plaun, who's been quiet.

"Theoretically it is possible," he says. "But in practice? I doubt it. In theory it's possible to re-create everything if you have enough information. But in practice? No. On the other hand, we do know that people are working on it."

Lindvig protests. They've done calculations, he says. The computer would have to process more than eighty million polygons per second in order to draw a copy of a three-dimensional image accurate enough to fool the eye. That means about fifty times more computational power than the most powerful computers today.

I try to clear my thoughts while the two of them discuss this. Monique must have had something on "them," whoever they were. What was that "something"? The photograph, perhaps. The photograph in itself. Or the film. What if they thought I had the film?

As far as I can tell from both Lindvig and Stig Plaun, the future will be a game about decimals. And fractions. And algorithms. When the world as we know it becomes formulized into an artificial universe, it'll seem just as incomprehensible as it does today. Images will pour down like multicolored rain from satellites dotting the sky like prisms. We might be sitting here with just a sliver of the knowledge awaiting us.

"This thing is a weapon, isn't it?" I say.

"Not necessarily," says Plaun.

Lindvig holds his head.

"Stop it, Martin. What you're imagining can't be done."

I ignore Lindvig's protests, for I can tell that Plaun isn't ruling it out. I look at him.

"It *is* a weapon, isn't it? The photograph, the film. The technology itself is a weapon!"

"Very hard to say. Because we don't know how it works. But if it works, then, yes, potentially it is a weapon."

We've seen it ourselves. We're sitting here looking at it. Her hair is a salvo of precisely calculated values; her skin the sum of a series of mutated numbers; her smile and mouth billions of dots, which only in the depth of the resolution of the image can be detected as a forgery, and only because someone made a stupid mistake. We're watching the first synthetic actress. And discussing whether she'd be able to walk. It's too unreal.

Lindvig comes over and grabs hold of me. It's as if he wants to explain a simple mathematical problem to someone autistic whom he has no hope of reaching. For a moment he considers raising the level of difficulty of the problem to get his point across.

"Look at me, Martin. It isn't possible." He repeats the words, slowly, staccato: "It just . . . isn't . . . possible."

Plaun shakes his head, as if to clear his head of a mirage.

"There are lots of 3-D simulation algorithms," he says. "Maybe they used a series of definitions from his body as a model. There's a very popular 3-D animation system, *Softimage*. I know it's solved the hierarchical problems in animation and given animators much more freedom and autonomy—they don't have to adjust separate parts manually anymore whenever they change something. But from there, it's still a leap. Also, we're not talking about a single program. This animation process would require a whole bunch of them."

He shakes his head.

"I just don't know. It's impossible to say."

"Listen," says Lindvig. "It's one thing to create single scenes and sequences in a movie. We've already seen that. But what we're talking about here is the complete animation of a human being. The basics alone: gravity, all the muscle groups that need to be governed by the calculations. The skin. Just think of the amount of time needed to calculate moving skin. Light and shadow on skin."

Lindvig looks at Plaun expectantly, as if he's waiting for him to give in. But Plaun doesn't. He picks up the photograph and hands it to me.

"I don't want to make any guesses. Not one way or the other. I've seen something that resembles this, but I don't want to say any more about it; I've been completely wrong before when I tried to make prophecies in data technology. Is there an American connection here, too?"

I nod.

"I'd look closer into that connection. You go to movies. So do I. There's no doubt who could make this kind of thing if it could be done. Assuming our guess is correct, it must have taken weeks, maybe months, even if there are only a few seconds' worth of film. I have no problems with the manipulations. If they really have the algorithms to make the initial one, they can easily handle the others. But if the time frame is as you've described, then it must have been done here in Denmark."

"Do you know of a company called DiaData?" I say.

"It's a service agency. They make a lot of television commercials. But I very much doubt that they'd be mixed up in something like this."

"Why?"

"Even if we ignore fact that they might have had something to do with the girl's death, the manipulation itself is illegal. And any movie made from it is worthless."

"Worthless?"

He collects his things on the table. As he clicks down the windows, I notice that he erases the scanned-in photograph from the directory. Lindvig is farther away, so he doesn't notice. Plaun turns off the table lamp and then the computer. Then he stands up.

"When I told you the resolution in the picture was lousy, it wasn't quite true. Compared to ordinary TV signals, it's actually twice as good. I assume that we all agree on the nature of the film: pornography. Okay. Porno is made to sell. To send. But this film can't be shown anywhere."

Lindvig looks at him skeptically. I stare with my mouth open.

"Why on earth not?"

"Because it can't be shown in this form at all. Not yet, anyway. What you have here is digital high-definition TV. HDTV."

It's a weird sensation to feel the future becoming real. Outside, the night is fading; everything seems normal. Light is rising in the southeast. Like the first layer of a gradual process of applying color and light, a thin layer of blue has lowered over the distant buildings. The buildings are still dark, but day will soon be dawning.

It'll take a few years. Only a few years. We shouldn't be thinking about it; it can drive you crazy. It's unreal only if you think about it. Once we're actually there, we won't feel like this. That's the power and major premise of progress and the future: you get used to them gradually. In a few years a waterfall of images will be pouring down from satellites. In a few years we'll all be gods producing the images we want to see, and want others to see. Preferably everyone.

Twenty-five pictures per second, unrolled one at a time in a regular tempo, is all it takes to convince us that they're actually one continuous movement. This is the principle used in the new digital TV. You cancel the data the human eye can't register and, since only parts of TV pictures actually change from frame to frame, all you need to send is data about the difference between each frame. Even in violent scenes, the eye won't be able to tell the difference.

As we walk back through the building toward the exit, Stig Plaun locks the glass doors behind us. He's walking fast, seems to be in a hurry.

"Consider this evening on the house, assuming that there'll never be anything said about it. Any place. Ever. To anyone."

"What's wrong?"

"What do you think?"

"You're the expert."

He looks straight ahead.

"Who do you think spends fortunes on things that apparently

are never intended to be used commercially? We're not talking about small change here. Who do you think can afford this?"

As we walk through the hallway, I'm trying to keep up with him. Lindvig lags a little behind.

"I'm afraid my imagination fails me," I say.

He smiles crookedly.

"I didn't think reporters had any problem with imagination," he says. "Who spends billions of dollars on technological research? Who conducted the last big war like a video game? Who orchestrated a rain of bombs with millimeter precision by simulator-trained soldiers? Who might need this? Who do you think might want to scramble enemy signals with phony video images? Who might gain time by blowing life into a dead dictator? And who might want to win a world with the aid of images?"

"You can't really mean that," I say.

"I don't mean a bloody thing. Remember that."

We get to the door. He holds it open while we wait for Lindvig to catch up.

"Why did you delete it?" I say.

"Because I didn't want it."

"Who's Jack Roth Pascal?"

He shakes his head. "Never heard of him," he says. Lindvig doesn't see it, but I do. I know right away that Plaun's lying.

It's getting light as we drive back through the city. Sunbeams are filling the streets. The day is coming without anyone asking us if we want it. Just like all progress. For better or worse, progress is coming. What's new is that no one's asking if we need it, if it will make us happier. What's new is that we don't even discuss it. If anyone objects, he'll be met with a steamroller of arguments about all the advantages. And if he really resists, they'll point to the lowest common denominator and our most basic fears: the fear of losing, of losing the people we love, of growing older, of dying. They've done it before and they'll do it again. Only after we've given in and learned to live with the New Order will we see that the so-called advantages were just arguments designed to camouflage the disadvantages, and the disadvantages are all we'll really be able to feel.

For a long time we ride in silence. Lindvig is searching for words but can't find any.

"Who's going to control it all, Lindvig?"

"What do you mean?"

"The images? The future? Your future?"

"I'm not sure I understand."

"Digital television. Manipulation of TV images."

"It's illegal."

"But how are we going to control it if we can't tell the difference? How are we going to be able to watch the news and know what's real and what isn't? And what about the soup of images everyone's plucking out of the air? Who knows what's been manipulated and what hasn't?"

"You heard what he said, Martin. How far-fetched the whole thing is. It's still possible that the photograph is genuine. You don't know anything for sure."

"That's the basic premise for everything, isn't it? That there's always a shadow of a doubt."

We drive through the city as the blue evening light dissipates. I knew Monique. She knew me. People grow connected to each other. They undergo a metamorphosis, and begin to melt into each other, to look alike. I know what I know. I know that they made a movie with Monique in which she took no part. I know that she found out what they could do, and that she wanted to stop them. I know that they showed her the movie and used it as blackmail. I know that in a panic she tried to change her looks, and I also know that shortly afterward she received a photo from the same film but with her new face. That's what I know.

I stop the car in front of Lindvig's apartment.

"Well, at least you learned something," he says. "Now you know how the technology can be used."

"Mostly how it can be misused."

Across the city on the corner of Nørrebrogade by the Assistens Cemetery, I stop at the side of the road and go into a phone booth. I get the number from the woman at Information and punch in the numbers. It rings and I wait. Finally someone picks up. A sour, sleepy voice says:

"There's no Stig Plaun at this number."

"Really? What number did I call?"

"That's for you to know."

"How can I know that if I called the wrong number?" I shout.

I slam down the receiver. I'm fuming. I press the keys slowly so I'll be sure to do it right. That's when I notice the bag on the floor of the booth. I bend down and pick it up while I press the receiver to my ear. The call goes through, but the number's busy. I hang up and open the bag, which contains a pair of gloves and a bottle cap. A strange sensation of déjà vu: I've been here before. I've stood this way before. It's as if it's been stored in my head the whole time, but only now do I realize where. In the airport, when Natasha gave me the shopping bag she wanted me to take through customs.

The tarps covering Kubjec's apartment are flapping in the wind. In the morning light the street is deserted. Little gusts of wind grab the material and tear at it like a soul trying to free itself. As if something is not quite dead yet. Kubjec is a mystery. I still can't find a place for him.

It's a clear morning. The day promises high sun and blue sky. Right now light is darting in among the buildings as through the cracks of an old wall. There are no people in the street, no sounds except from the tarps that flap in the wind and the metal fittings that bang against the scaffolding.

Tired and dizzy, I walk up to the apartment. I try calling Plaun again. It's still busy.

I hang up. Angrily I start guzzling straight whiskey until I feel that I'm going to throw up. I feel I have a right to smash everything in the room. No doubt I'm worsening the fracture in my hand, but every time I connect with my skinned knuckles and something breaks, I feel better. Then I start searching.

I go through everything. Drawers, dressers, closets. I tear the kitchen drawers out of their gliders and noisily drop utensils all over the floor, I scour all possible cracks along panels and doors and window frames. I take out Monique's coats and spread them on the living-room floor. First I go through them carefully, then I get a kitchen knife and cut the fabric, at first gingerly, as if the coats were alive, then more violently; finally I rip and tear at the linings, the pockets, the inner pockets and collars. Then I start on the living room. Pull out furniture, rip open cushions and throw them in all directions.

Finally I attack the bookcase. It teeters for moment, then I kick it again. With a huge crash it hits the windowsill and breaks in the middle, sending records, tapes, and CDs all over the floor. It's not there. Not this time either. It was there, Monique, but now it's gone. In the bag from Natasha there was a CD, and *you* brought back a Vivaldi CD which is not there anymore.

I collapse on the couch and rewind the video a few times. The nurse is on the bed, Nikolai Martin behind her. I stop it. Rewind slowly. Freeze the picture. There. Exactly as in the picture. Sweat dripping from his eyes. Out of him they created Monique. The rib of Adam. Nikolai Martin doesn't even know it. He had nothing to do with it.

She's awake when I call.

"Don't you think we should talk a little now?"

"About what? It's not what you think at all."

"I don't know what I think."

"Go to bed, Martin. Call me one day when you're normal."

"Is he there now? Are you fucking right now?"

"Oh, stop it."

"Do you like to swallow his sperm, Natasha?"

"Martin!"

"Some women say it tastes like egg."

"Martin."

"Of course it may be because of the cholesterol."

I sleep all day. Only when it begins to grow dark do I get up and get dressed. It's evening, Danish time, but they're waking up in Los Angeles. I call Barbra in the *Los Angeles Times* archives.

She laughs loudly when she's heard me out.

"Industrial espionage, you say? Could you be a bit more specific?"

"Using computers."

"That's a dime a dozen. I'll turn you over to Yul Morris. He knows everything about computers."

Morris tells me that the FBI had to establish a special office in Silicon Valley. Last week they caught a German in the San Francisco airport with a diskette in his pocket.

"It contained the source code of a computer program used in the defense industry," he says.

"But aren't there limits to how much a small diskette can hold?"

"With all the new compression tools? Not really. The real problem is that today most companies are connected to networks the way they used to be connected to mainframes."

"But why not simply tap the system from outside? Isn't that safer?"

"Quite the contrary. When you're on the inside, all you have to do is put a diskette into the PC. Obviously there are safeguards—codes and all that—but it's amazing how often an intrusion doesn't get discovered."

"But when it's a question of large amounts of data, I suppose they can break it down into sections and then transfer it to CD-ROMs?"

"Well, it's not so easy to *store* the stuff on CDs."

"Some people must be able to."

"In cases like that we're talking about some form of organized trafficking. Hypothetically speaking, CDs are better than diskettes, but there's a lot of research being done to compress data further onto disks. Actually, they just need to find a way to make the tracks on the disk narrower. Narrower track width means room for more data. What exactly is this all about?"

"An American who's been systematically stealing data."

"Sounds strange. The biggest problem is usually with foreign groups working here. Is he taking the information to sell it outside the country?"

I can hear something—maybe a tape recorder—being connected to the phone. One reporter pumping another. I decide not to say any more.

"I don't have all the details in place yet," I say.

"The reason I'm asking is, as you probably know, Clinton and Gore are pouring endless amounts of money into the computer industry. You'd think that would make it more advantageous to do the developing in this country."

"Or maybe they've discovered how much is disappearing."

When it gets dark, I go out. The house is hidden away in a small, quiet section of Sorgenfri, a Copenhagen suburb, single-family homes. The driveway is empty and the house is dark.

I drive to the next crossroad, turn and park the car. Then I walk back to the house.

It's a yellow-brick, two-story corner house with a view of the fields down to Frederiksdal and Fure Lake. I follow the path around the house and peek in the windows that face the road, but there's nothing to see. I turn the corner and step onto the south terrace, where an awning has been rolled out halfway so that it's shading a table and some chairs. Behind the window is a living room with an open fireplace in darkness. When I've walked all around the house, I position myself against the front wall, hidden by some bushes and the garage. I wait.

After about a half hour he appears. I duck as headlights sweep across the house's facade and the car heads into the garage. The driver turns off the engine, leaves the garage, and walks up the garden path.

"Plaun," I say. "Stig Plaun."

He's startled, but when he sees me, he quickly comes over to me.

"Idiot," he says.

"What's that supposed to mean?"

He motions for me to be quiet, then pulls me by the coat sleeve, and together we inch our way down the wall of the house.

At that moment the Mazda turns into the road. Black and shiny, it glides past the hedge as quietly as a shark.

"They've been following me all day," he says. "What the hell are you doing here?"

"I have to know more about him."

"I don't know any more," he says.

"Yes, you do. I know you do."

He looks at me, annoyed. Then he whispers:

"Not here." He looks around. "I'm going to go inside and turn on the lights. Meet me behind the house in a few minutes."

I stand at the end of the house for a while, but when light suddenly pours from the window, I duck. Just at that moment the black Mazda passes by again. I wait a little longer, then walk around to the back of the house.

We take a series of paths that wind among clusters of neighboring row houses.

"What exactly do you want to know?" he says.

I stop.

"Who is Jack Roth Pascal?"

"Keep walking," he says. We move a little farther down the path. In the distance we can see a woman walking her dog. Otherwise, no one's around.

"It's a damn uncomfortable situation you've put me in," he says. "Are they following you too?"

I nod. A car passes on the street at the end of the path. Even though it's not the black Mazda, Plaun presses up against the hedge. It occurs to me that the man is quite frightened.

"Don't you think it's peculiar that you know so little about him?" he says. "I assume you've had searches done on him?"

I nod again.

"One can look for information or remove information. No information is also information. That ought to tell you something."

"I know he's worked for something called TDI," I say. "What is TDI?"

"TDI was a splinter group from Thomson."

"Thomson? The electronics company?"

"Together with Philips they were in the race to develop the American digital standard for high-definition TV. The engineers who broke with Thomson a few years ago at first established a production extension of Thomson: TDI, Thomson Digital Images. They developed the software program *Explore*. It's been a great success here in Europe, especially in France, but some of their programs are also used in Hollywood. At some point IBM bought in to acquire the know-how for a RISC-based system. The marriage didn't work. IBM developed their own version, but it didn't work as well for the Silicon Graphics computers as the other version. I don't know what the status of it all is now, but some of the engineers were so dissatisfied at the end that they backed out. However, they did have time to develop some pretty extraordinary rendering techniques that made it possible to go into separate parts of a scene and do rendering without having to run the program for the whole scene. Jack Roth Pascal was one of the engineers who jumped ship."

"What else do you know about him?"

"At one point a few years ago, there were rumors that a computer expert cracked some codes to NSA's cryptography system."

"NSA?"

"National Security Agency. Everyone knows that Jack Roth Pascal was the one under suspicion."

I take out Stella's list. In the faint light from the streetlamp I go through it.

"I don't see anything about NSA in here."

"That's because the case was never made public. In the old days NSA was called No Such Agency because the American government insisted that it didn't exist. Today it has a central place among the various intelligence services. It's a highly sophisticated technological agency responsible for international supervision of data communication; it monitors, unscrambles, and deciphers international codes. It's the modern CIA.

"All this unscrambling business started in earnest during World War Two. Every country used codes. This was the age of crystal detectors. During the Cold War, the Americans refined the unscrambling techniques. You spoke, before, of image manipulation as a weapon. Unscrambling keys are also weapons, to such a degree, in fact, that American companies aren't allowed to export algorithms because they're classified as weapons. That went into effect back in the Cold War, but it's still in place. It stops American companies from selling unscrambling software for millions of dollars. And this annoys them. I can't really blame them. After all, everything is a question of algorithms. Data turned into nonsense. Anybody can do it. Only now it's all the other countries who can sell them and make the profit."

"And Jack Roth Pascal is supposed to be the one who cracked the NSA codes?"

He nods. "A pretty embarrassing situation for a security agency that's in charge of filtering and decoding communication signals."

"But is it really possible to decode the signals?"

"I doubt it, but I don't know. All I know is that it would take enormous expertise and a huge amount of data power. The unscrambling keys built into the American surveillance satellites are so extensive that it takes twenty-four hours just to download them. And the access key is changed once a day. All this is crackling around in the sky above us. There are computers that do nothing but create and send access keys out into space. The more likely explanation is that the old algorithms were deliberately leaked in order to make sure personnel was still needed to get rid of the old ones and install the new ones. NSA is one of the biggest employers in Maryland, and jobs are hard to come by."

"But if he's broken their system, you wouldn't think he was their best friend."

"That's not the way it works. Business associations aren't usually created out of friendship. More likely out of fear."

I light a cigarette. The flame flares up in the darkness, and I feel him studying me intently.

"Do you know of any connection between Pascal and Dia-Data?" he asks.

"Not yet. Does the name Kubjec tell you anything? Tom

Kubjec?"

He shakes his head.

"Kubjec worked at DiaData. He's dead. I'm pretty sure he was murdered."

"Do you tell everyone you talk to that the people you've talked to are dead?"

"I never talked to Kubjec."

"And that's how you reassure them? That the ones you haven't talked to are dead, too?"

We follow the path to the house for a few blocks until it divides.

"Who did you talk to on the phone yesterday morning?" I say.

He stops.

"What the hell is that to you?"

"It was right after we'd been together."

"My wife," he says. "She has family in Australia. That's where she is now. But you really have a problem if you can't tell friends from enemies."

"I thought you said there are no such things as friends."

He smiles. We continue down the path.

"You said you'd seen examples of image manipulation that looked like this one. What were they?"

"Did I say they looked like this one? They didn't. Compared to what you showed me, you could call them dry runs. But the intent was very clear. Do you remember during the Gulf War when the allies were looking for Hussein? Do you remember when no one knew if he was alive or dead? Just imagine a future in which a country's leaders always seem beyond the reach of its citizens. You spoke of image manipulation as a weapon. If they really have developed a program that can manipulate live images as fast as you said this one worked, then they have a real weapon. Digital material can be changed ad infinitum, and no one can tell. Digital copies are as good as the original. In fact, the digital process changes the whole relationship between copy and original. From now on there *are* no originals, only copies. Take Rodney King, for instance. What if that taping was a fake? What if someone had messed around with it?"

I try to sound like Lindvig. Skeptical. In order to make him speak. I need to know everything he knows.

"There will probably be restrictions against using that kind of material in a court of law," I say. "And for the time being, court cases are still decided in court houses."

"Are they? What about the Rodney King case? Wasn't television the real judge? What if, theoretically, the videotape in which the officers beat him had been manipulated?"

"Well, there's always journalistic integrity."

He laughs. Loudly. I join him. We walk the last few steps along the path, then go into a crouch again just before the house. The black Mazda is gone.

"Why are you so fascinated by all this?" I ask.

He smiles. Then gets a distant, almost dreamy expression in his eyes.

"When I was a boy, one day I discovered that the sky wasn't really blue. I read that we merely experience it as blue, because the atmosphere refracts away all light from the sun except the blue. Ever since then it's been clear to me that everything is an illusion. And since then I've been obsessed with illusions. The most important thing is to acknowledge beauty and preserve the ability to be fascinated. If you can see the beauty even in what you most despise, you have a chance of mastering it."

We stand there for a while. In the distance, behind the hedges, you can make out the flickering light from Farum on the other side of Fure Lake.

"This is where our paths separate," he says, and looks at me regretfully. "And you might as well know where you stand: I never saw that photograph, and if it ever comes up in any way, I'll deny it."

"Fair enough."

He pauses, as if thinking about something.

"Do they just keep tailing you?"

I nod.

"Have you ever considered how easily you could be removed if they wanted to?"

"What do you mean by that?"

"The photo falsification wasn't actually all that difficult to see. Have you ever considered that they want to keep you alive. That someone *wants* you to discover all this?"

Chapter Seventeen

When we stop being deluged by images every time we close our eyes. When we stop imagining that we sense more than our immediate thoughts. When we stop remembering—a great, dark, blessed forgetfulness—only then will we have a chance for happiness, mainly because we won't know any better.

She calls the next morning. She's completely changed. Cold. Aggressive.

"You called my mother."

"Yes . . ."

"What did you say to her?"

"Nothing."

"What did she say?"

"Nothing."

"I'll never forgive you," she says.

I say, "Am *I* the one you'll never forgive?"

The house, big and white, grips the top of a hill that slopes down to a small forest beyond which lie the beach and the ocean.

It's late afternoon. A cool sea breeze bathes the road. People move lazily up the path on their way home. The atmosphere is peaceful, as if a carnival has just left town.

Natasha is sleeping in the sun. On her forehead tiny, pearly drops of sweat glisten, almost twinkle like a veil of diamonds. As she lies there on the grass surrounded by a sea of miniature white daisies, the scene looks like a curiously exotic coronation. Or the funeral of an angel.

As I walk down the garden path, she sits up, squinting. On the lawn next to her are a white table and chairs shaded by a blue parasol. She gets up and slips into a thin white dress.

"What do you want?" she says.

"To talk. Are you alone?"

"Aren't we all?"

She goes to the table and parasol. "About what?"

"I have some questions."

She pours a glass for herself. Then turns toward me. "What do you want?"

"Answers."

Sipping from her glass, she faces me directly. She puts the glass down and lights a cigarette.

"Why, Martin?"

"Because it's important."

"To whom?"

Right here by the honeysuckle hedge, under tall, frayed pines, on this sparkling green lawn, Natasha has talked to and made love to people I don't know. I don't know her past. She's a stranger just as Monique was a stranger. There are places in each other we never manage to reach.

In the white pavilion below the house, she's danced at summer parties, in warm, embracing darkness, with faces I've never seen. And here on this lawn she's wrapped herself in lovers whom she herself may not remember anymore. In an upstairs bedroom from whose window a white down comforter hangs like a soft tongue, she's slept, dreamed, and been frightened by things I know nothing about.

Something shaped her, made her into the person she is. Lindvig says it's all a question of codes—that it's programmed into us from the beginning, and there's nothing we can do about it. We're nothing but a rehash, a stew of other people's unhappiness. It's only now—because of computers—that we're finally beginning to understand this.

I look at her polished red nails, as hard, shiny, and pointy as ice picks. When she pulls the white fabric taut in the grip of lovemaking, her nails can cut through sheets.

"Natasha, what's the best way to conceal a CD?"

"What do you mean?"

"*On* a CD," I say, answering my question.

"I don't know what you're talking about."

"It's really very simple, isn't it? I'm talking about the bag, Natasha."

"The bag?"

"The CD in the bag you gave me."

"What about it?"

"What was on it?"

"Music."

I smile.

"Don't you believe me?" she says. "Do you want me to get it?"

For a fraction of a second I'm unsure.

"But I know how it works now," I say.

"Do you, Martin? Do you really?"

"They're codes. You're smuggling program codes into the country. Monique did the same thing, didn't she?"

"I have no idea what you're talking about."

I walk to the table and pour myself a drink.

"What about the photograph?" I say.

"What photograph?"

"The photograph you were looking for."

"I have no idea what you're talking about."

"It couldn't have been anyone but you."

"What do you want to do about it, Martin?"

"Why did you want the photograph?"

"I have no idea which idiotic photograph you're talking about."

I grab her.

"Don't you, Natasha? Don't you really?"

"Let go of me," she says.

"Who's paying you, Natasha? Who pays for this?" I wave my arm around. "For all of this!"

"Let go of me, goddammit. You're out of your mind!"

I hit her. Her hair stands like a shower around her face. She brushes it away, then slowly turns her head and looks at me, her eyes narrow.

"You're a dirty whore," I say.

"You never paid for it."

I hit her again, hard.

"Didn't I, Natasha?"

I let go of her, and she falls limply onto the grass. She's crying.

"There's nothing you can do about it, Martin."

"What do you mean?"

"They're after you."

She gets up, shakily. The whole tableau is bewilderingly beautiful: the white villa up the hill in the last golden sun, its chest pushed forward as if defying the ocean.

"I saw you in the hotel in Los Angeles."

"What did you see, Martin?"

"You went into room 505."

"What about it?"

"He was in there, wasn't he? He was there."

"I can't help you, Martin."

She stands in front of me, an enigma whose secrets I can't penetrate and solve.

"We never really connect with each other, do we?"

She looks at me with narrowed eyes.

"What do you mean?"

"I mean just that."

Then I walk back to my car. Behind me I see her standing on the lawn, her white dress flapping in the last breeze of the day.

Following sheer impulse, I call DiaData that afternoon. I've got to establish a firm connection between Tom Kubjec and Jack Roth Pascal. I want to be sure. Absolutely sure.

After I've introduced myself, I inform them that I've examined the company's records on *Publicom* and that I'd like to check some details.

"I'll transfer you," she says. "You have to speak to Vivi Fleiss."

There's a considerable pause before I'm reconnected, long enough for a quick briefing—assuming the receptionist knows her job.

"Vivi Fleiss."

I introduce myself again. Explain what I want. I make up a story.

"I can't tell from the accounts whether Jack Roth Pascal is a stockholder with more than ten percent, so I'm interested in getting an up-to-date record."

"If a stockholder isn't registered in our latest report, then he probably wouldn't be now either."

"Well, he might have bought more stock recently, for instance," I suggest.

"Why are you interested in this information?" she says. She hasn't taken the bait. Not yet. She's on guard and alert. "I'm not even sure you're entitled to it."

I'm banking on the fact that she doesn't know that paragraph 28a, section 2, of the corporate statutes requires a written request for this kind of information.

"According to the law, I am," I say.

She hesitates.

"Listen," she says, "there's no reason to make a big deal of this. I'll personally vouch for the fact that Jack Roth Pascal doesn't own any stock in the company at all. Why are you so interested?"

"I'm not. I just wanted to know if you knew him."

DiaData is only one stitch in a net, and the net is a jumble of smaller nets. In the future, the cables of the information highway will sputter and hiss with signals sent from centrally located superservers—the pulsating hearts of the new digital world.

From Information I get the number for Tele Trois. A media giant with solid investments in a smaller French telecommunication company as well as in a long list of electronics companies, it's situated a little outside of Paris.

I hesitate a moment, then call. Push a few buttons. It's all become so easy.

I present myself as Jack Roth Pascal and ask to speak to the director of the company, Maurice Dubiac. I say I'm in a hurry. I'm put through right away.

"Dubiac."

I introduce myself as myself.

"The press? Then you'll want our PR department. I was told it was someone else."

"Just a moment, Monsieur Dubiac. He's actually the person I want to speak to you about."

"I'm not sure I understand."

"Jack Roth Pascal," I say.

"I'm sorry, but I don't discuss any of our consultants with the press."

"It concerns the product he's been developing at DiaData in Denmark."

"I'm sorry, but you'll have to speak to our PR department . . ."

"I've seen something of what the program is capable of, and I'm just wondering for whom it's designed. Who's going to buy it?"

"I'm afraid you know more than I do. I'm not up on the technical side of things. I only know that there's an exciting product on its way from the Danish developers."

"But what about the codes for the programs? It must have taken years to develop them . . ."

"I'm sorry, but . . ."

"Or did they come with the TDI engineers? And what about *Softimage*? Did they contribute to it too without knowing it?"

"Monsieur Pascal has a network of brilliant advisors, but I

hope you're not suggesting that any illegalities have been committed."

"Was he also the one to tell you not to screw up the way Thomson, Philips, and the Japanese did? You could have had millions from the EC if you'd gone along with HDMAC. So why didn't you? Did Pascal let you know what was on the way from General Instruments?"

"What do you mean?"

"Digicipher. The compression of digital TV signals."

"Our company has a right to be farsighted. Everyone knows that the future will be digital. But aside from that, I don't care for your tone. Simulation and animation programs aren't illegal, and whom will it harm, may I ask, to create digital actors? If we don't do it, someone else certainly will."

"So you do know the product?"

"I don't want to be quoted on any of this," he says.

"If you trust Jack Roth Pascal so much, don't you wonder why you haven't seen the finished program yet?"

"What do you mean?"

"The program from DiaData is ready to go."

He's silent now. But curious enough to keep listening.

"And don't you wonder why people are getting killed because of that program?"

After a short pause, he says, "I have no idea what you're talking about." Then the connection is cut. I sit for a while with the singing receiver in my hand.

You have no idea what I'm talking about—but then why hang up the phone?

It's early evening, and we've already had most of the day that they're waking up to in Los Angeles.

Preventive measures don't come naturally to human beings. Prevention is an irrational process. And humans are rational. To the point when it begins to pay to be irrational. Rationally speaking. No one will benefit from preventing an accident which remains invisible to the eye. We pollute and then clean up. We blunder and then deny it. It's in our nature. We want to see the consequences of our deeds. Even if they're misdeeds.

We're like beaten animals.

When I die, will my heart be worn out by disease or exhaustion? Or by lack of love? Will hers?

I should have asked her about her sorrows. Her defeats, her endless list of disappointments.

Perhaps that might have changed everything. I don't know. I think about Monique. And I think about Natasha. About the words.

These days anyone can call the NSA. I get the telephone number and address from the overseas operator. National Security Agency, Fort Meade, Maryland. Nothing's kept secret today. On the surface. Something's out in the open, and somehow that makes us believe that everything really is.

"Are you calling from a secure line, sir?"

"Excuse me?"

"All overseas calls must be checked. Are you calling from a secure line?"

Suddenly I'm in doubt. I study the receiver. Turn over the carriage. Look around the room. I have no idea. I have absolutely no idea.

I hang up.

I call the Four Seasons. I ask for Louis.

"If Jack Roth Pascal checks in, you have to promise to call me. He may use the name Jacob Roth Pascal."

"I'm sorry, sir. I can't give you any information about our guests."

"Louis! Louis, it's me, Molberg!"

"I know, sir."

For a moment I'm confused. Then I say:

"He's there now? Louis, is that what you mean?"

"That's right, sir. Good-bye."

I start packing, pouring the whole box of Monique's old letters into the suitcase. I don't want to leave anything behind for Klinker. Everything might end up in a battle over words. Over circumstantial evidence. Over interpretation of a few old letters and notes.

I pick out a simple place for the photograph. They've been in the apartment already; if they come back, most likely they'll break up the floor and rip down the wallpaper. But they'll never think to look under a couch cushion.

I pack a few clothes, then get the tear-gas capsule from the shelf in my workroom. I experiment a bit. With a little effort it can fit into a pack of cigarettes when half of the cigarettes have been taken out. In a pinch, it might pass for a lighter.

I stand by the window. The houses seem to have moved closer together, as though they're shivering from the cold. I lean against the sill. I'm tired and feverish. My hands are bony, and I feel I'm about to vomit. Obsessive-compulsive is what Dr. Phillip would call me. My face is warm from the setting sun, which spreads its apricot color on the walls of distant buildings. The way I pace by the window, anyone watching me from the houses across the street would see me as a restless ghost in a tower. The tarps from the destroyed apartment wave in the wind, and in the backyard across the street a lovesick cat is howling. It'll be doing that next year, too. The first leaves are falling, and they'll be doing that next year, too. It'll all go on and on. Endlessly.

Night after night a stranger out there was emptying himself into the woman I loved. Statistically, at least twice a week. Who was he? Jack Roth Pascal? And who was he? Who is he? Did you end your life in his arms, Monique? I don't know. When all is said and done, I just don't know.

It was the little things. It's always the little, insignificant things that grow and change everything. Strange telephone calls that used to be merely private suddenly began to seem suspect. An illness, a poison, had been introduced and started to spread. Or was it all an incorrect diagnosis? Unimportant events in the past suddenly gained new significance. When she wore a scarf on a spring day, was she really ill? Or was she hiding a mark—a small, unimportant violet mark—as if skin alone would reveal the body's betrayal.

A childhood incident that finally came to the fore? Mother? Father? Monique? Wasn't she just simple proof of the sad fact that sooner or later we all betray each other? It goes on and on.

I call Klinker. He picks up the phone himself.

"I know who did it," I say. "I know who killed Monique. I also know who killed young Kubjec."

"I'm glad you called, Molberg. We also want to talk to *you* about the explosion in number sixteen."

"Do you think I did that too?"

"What were you doing when it happened?"

"I was awake. I woke up. I saw something."

"Were you alone?"

"No, I have a witness."

"I see. The girl? Natasha Noiret?"

"Yes. But I don't suppose she'll do, will she? You think I killed Kubjec, just as I killed my own girlfriend?"

"As a matter of fact, we still have a few questions about that too."

"What about my witness? Doesn't that still count?"

He's silent for a moment.

"But Molberg," he says, surprised. "I thought you knew. Kubjec *was* your witness."

Chapter Eighteen

Palms spread their wings across the entrance to the egg-yolk-colored hotel. Under the large, flat awning reporters and photographers wait. Heavyset bodyguards in suits clear the way for Mr. Nicholson and his wife, who floats along in his aura. The sun has made dappled freckles on her skin, and although she's covered them with powder, close up they look like a faint belt of dots, DNA drawings under her skin. He's wearing dark sunglasses and smiling his famous smile.

Press people are crushing up against them while the hotel staff rushes around in their white jackets and black pants. In a group of foreign film critics I spot Jan Borris.

"Molberg! Hi!" he says. When I try to slip past him, he pulls my sleeve. "Meet Ursula."

A smiling, rather chubby woman comes over.

"*Wer ist er?*"

"Martin, *ein alter Freund,*" Borris says. "Have you said hello to your old friend Nicholson? He was just here. But perhaps you arrived together."

Without quite being aware of it, I shake hands with the smiling German reporter.

"I don't have time for this, Jan."

"They're asking for you at the paper. What should I say if they ask if I've seen you?"

"Tell them I'm working. Jan, I'm in a hurry."

"Making up more stories?"

I tear myself away. "Let go of me, damn it, or I'll kill you."

He throws his hands up defensively. "Well, excuse me."

"*Bild Zeitung*," says the smiling Ursula to a female colleague who's joined us.

"*Durch, für, gegen,*" I say, and push brutally between them.

In my room I break two Dexedrines and rinse them down with whiskey from the bar cabinet. Then I reach for the remote and turn the sound up high on the large TV to blast myself awake: I'm here to kill a man. I'm here to find out what happened during the last hours of Monique Milazar's life. From the only person who can tell me. And then to kill him. As simple as that. I know his name but have no idea who he is or what he looks like. The sound from the TV doesn't change a thing: my intention isn't a fantasy any longer. Nothing can stop me now.

I call room service and ask for Louis.

"He's not here, Mr. Molberg."

"Who am I speaking to?" I say.

"This is Steven, sir. How can I help you, Mr. Molberg?"

"When will Louis be getting here?"

"He isn't coming," Steven says. "He left a number for you to call, Mr. Molberg. Do you have a pen?"

"Don't you usually send up messages?"

He speaks quietly.

"Yes, but this is a bit against regulations. I'm just doing Louis a favor. He's been having some problems, but you better speak to him yourself."

"What's happened?"

"Better call him yourself, Mr. Molberg. I may get in trouble for this, too."

He reads me the number.

"What kind of problems?"

But he hangs up. I write down the number and hang up.

When I call, Louis is home.

"What's happened?" I say.

"They found out. I got fired."

"I'm sorry about that."

"Don't be, Mr. Molberg. I just wish you'd told me what this was all about from the beginning."

"I didn't know at the time, Louis. I honestly didn't know."

"This Jack Roth Pascal is a real son of a bitch, isn't he?"

"Yes," I say. "It all has to do with a murder of a woman."

"Well, I hope she was really important to you."

"Listen, Louis, I'd very much like to pay you for all the trouble I've caused."

"That's not what I was talking about," he says.

"What *are* you talking about?"

"You're in trouble, Mr. Molberg. Big trouble."

I find my pack of cigarettes and knock one out. I light it and inhale.

"Talk to me, Louis."

"First, let me tell you what he looks like so you can find him.

For the last couple of days, usually about an hour from now, he's been eating dinner with various guests in the hotel restaurant. There's a good chance that he'll be doing the same today; if not, he's in room 505. He has at least two people around him, either close friends or bodyguards. He's a little taller than me, about six-two, in his late thirties I'd say. If you can't recognize him any other way, just look at his hands. From his wrist and across his fingers he's got scars on both hands. It doesn't look like a skin disease, more like burns. As if the skin melted."

"You have a good memory, Louis."

"When you work in room service, you notice people's hands, Mr. Molberg. You were generous; Mr. Pascal is a bad tipper."

"I'd like to send you some money, Louis."

"I think it's safer if we have no more contact, Mr. Molberg. I'm going up to stay with some friends in San Francisco tonight. Tomorrow I'll head for the East Coast."

"You're taking this very seriously."

"You should too, Mr. Molberg. Do you have a weapon?"

I don't have a weapon. All I have is the tear-gas capsule. It was the only thing I could think of that might clear security in the Copenhagen airport. I've thought a lot about how much actually gets through airport security. The foil wrappers in cigarette packs kick the alarms off so often that the guards don't notice anymore if you hand the packs around the detectors as you go through.

L'utilisateur est responsable de son usage, it says on the small capsule. Use at your own risk. That's all right with me. The liquid may not actually kill Pascal, but if it eats away his eyes and blinds him, I'll be content.

"I think I'll improvise," I say. "What kind of trouble am I in, Louis?"

"First of all, I've heard that I was fired by Jack Pascal himself and not by the hotel management. I have a feeling that's true. Supposedly it's grounds for firing if you give out information about a guest. Before the manager got rid of me, I had to go talk to Pascal alone. He wasn't rude or unpleasant, but he kept asking me what I knew about you, and why I'd looked up his name on the computer. The strange thing is that no one at the hotel mentioned that I'd looked up the woman's name, and that *that's* what was suspicious. That's the only thing they could have discovered. Looking up Pascal's name wasn't anything out of the ordinary—it's a daily procedure for all guests at the hotel. But since no one's mentioned the other thing, it must have been my checking on him that they discovered, which means that somehow he's surveying the whole computer system himself. But because I'd discovered something else about his account, I just told him that I'd looked him up because there'd been a call for him. That's how they caught me: Jack Roth Pascal doesn't receive any calls when he stays here. I didn't know that."

"What was it you discovered?"

"Who pays for his stay."

"Who?"

"There was a telephone number. I looked it up. It's the number of NSA."

On the fourth floor, there's a pool party for Mr. Nicholson's movie.

As I come out of the bathroom after a quick shower, I hear soft knocking at the door. It's not Steven but someone else from room service who hands me a silver tray with a drink and some snacks.

"Compliments of the hotel," he says. "We apologize for the

closing of the pool. It'll be closed only until the press is finished."

"That may be a while," I say.

I take the tray from him and hand him a bill. Then shut the door and place the silver tray on the bedside table. The curtains flutter faintly in the breeze from the open balcony door as the sun sets over Beverly Hills.

That night I burn the letters from Monique Milazar. I heave the suitcase up onto the bed, empty out all the papers I'd stuffed it with. Then I dump them into the bathroom waste basket.

I don't want to leave anything behind. No trace. No explanations.

I'd imagined happiness taking place in a world of lazily falling house dust, a world which one could furnish and protect simply by keeping the door closed. It's so easy to fool oneself.

When I think of what we might have been! Monique and I had a real chance at happiness—every chance, really. But all that seemed to emerge was the possibility of making more and more mistakes. We ignored the fact that we were responsible for each other because it was too much trouble, and discovered only too late that part of the responsibility had to do with ourselves. The responsibility we had to become happy.

We were young, beautiful, privileged.

We didn't realize that we needed to put limits on ourselves. Our possibilities seemed infinite. We chose to see the limits as yet another possibility. We thought happiness could be found in the things we chose to do instead of in the things we chose to do without. That was our mistake.

But I don't know if even this is true. It's words. Nothing more. We just think that there's a design to our lives.

"There *is* a design," Dr. Phillip stubbornly insists. But you can choose to see it that way when coincidences fall so close together that it looks like there's a pattern.

My head is swimming and I'm nauseous. I keep having to run to the bathroom to throw up. Maybe I'm getting sick. Or maybe it's just the booze. I force down the hotel drink.

Then everything short-circuits. Black sparks crackle in my head. Signals fade and images fall away, replaced by other images.

As Dr. Phillip says, there are two kinds of mourning: the kind that's relived through tears and commiseration. And my kind: big, black, repressed. Maybe now it's trying to get out. "It'll hit you even harder next time." Maybe he was right.

You've assured yourself a synthetic immortality, Monique. You'll crackle across thousands of screens in the New World. They've reconstructed you and given you eternal life in a world that unites the seemingly incompatible: numbers and images. You've become the sum total of other people's fantasies, a mathematical problem in the heads of sick people. And one day they may even find a way to reach your body. But maybe even when you were alive, you were already somewhere else.

My whole body feels faint and all my muscles ache. Like small exploding suns under my skin. Is it from tension? Or from sleeping with strange, random women like Natasha Noiret, whom I made love to as if we were old sweethearts trying to comfort each other.

This myriad of thoughts. This muddle of bits and pieces that don't fit together. Was it Monique's fault? Mother's? Father's? Mine? Who the fuck cares?

Monique was a part of me. I was a part of her. But perhaps we never really grew together. Perhaps I didn't give anything. Perhaps I had nothing to give. Perhaps I was so afraid of letting the madness out that I couldn't let anything else out. Including love. Which meant that only the madness got out.

I ought to get myself a weapon. A revolver or an automatic pistol. But I'm an idiot when it comes to guns. I always forget: does a revolver have a clip or a cylinder? I think a cylinder. In journalism school they drilled it into us that the details are what's important; the reader notices the mistakes. But I have no head for weapons; my best weapon is my rage. And my only strength is that I'm not afraid. I have nothing more to lose.

I throw a match into the waste basket. The papers curl and the blue ink shines in the flames. Black snow flutters around the charred balls of paper.

I turn on the tape recorder and tuck it into my inside jacket pocket. Then pick up the cigarette pack with the tear-gas capsule. And at that moment I collapse.

By the time I finally drag myself to the telephone and call Reception, I can hardly breathe.

"What was in the drinks?" I say.

"Drinks? What drinks?"

I hang up and struggle back to my feet. When I make it out to the hallway, it's as if I'm pulled by magnets toward the carpet. I crawl the first few feet, then get back up, staggering toward Jan Borris's door. He opens it himself.

"Molberg! What the hell do you want?"

I look past him into the room. German Ursula from *Bild Zeitung* is sitting on the bed.

"Did they give you drinks, too?"

I cling to the door frame while I slide slowly downward.

"What the hell is wrong with you? Are you drunk?"

"I don't feel very good."

I feel a jab in my gut and double up.

"Yes, we've had drinks too, but we didn't overdo it," he says, trying to push the door shut. I manage to wedge a foot in.

"Jan, I think I need a little help."

He looks at me contemptuously.

"You've needed help for a long time."

Then he pushes the door shut.

I knock, but he doesn't open. So I stand there swaying in the empty hotel hall, trying to focus, but it's impossible. Polygons are popping out of walls and plants are dancing down the hallway like streaks in the air. Details dissolve into graininess; all I can see is a soup of fat, engorged pixels. Everything's swimming.

I stagger as best I can toward the elevators. I have no idea what I've been drinking, but whatever it was, it's obvious that I won't be able to stay on my feet much longer. I take the elevator down to the lobby and manage to get out before the doors shut. As I struggle to push past a young couple waiting for the elevator, they smile knowingly. Everything's spinning.

If I manage to focus, I can keep myself up and inch slowly toward the bar and the restaurant while the surroundings whirl in my head. I feel flashes of heat as if someone is touching the back of my neck. My ears are clogged, and I'm aware of a loud, thundering sound. The dizziness is pushing me over, but I cling to the walls and make it to the entrance of the restaurant.

"Can I help you, sir?"

"I'm looking for Mr. Jack Pascal."

The waiter points toward the window.

"Just let me get another setting; I didn't realize they were expecting another guest."

"They weren't."

He measures me with his eyes.

"You look sick, sir."

"I am. Sick of all of you."

I sail among the tables in the direction of the people the waiter pointed out. As I tip into a serving table, a fork in my hand feels so good that I hold onto it. As I stagger closer, two people at the table get up, and when I leap, a shower of fists lands on my back while I slide across the tablecloth and dig the fork into his chest. I get a glimpse of a waiter rushing forward and hear someone saying: "Don't worry, he's with us. We'll take care of him." Then everything turns black.

I don't know what time it is, what day. I'm sitting on a soft striped couch in someone's suite. In the other room a man is sitting on the edge of the bed talking on the telephone; I recognize him as one of the two men I saw from my window back home. I'm not sure of the other sitting opposite me in a chair, he may have been the one in the Mazda. Through the sheer curtains I can just make out a figure on the balcony. It's getting dark, but I feel that it's still today. Faint music reaches us from the pool below.

The man who's been talking on the telephone puts it down and walks out onto the balcony. Then both men come back inside.

"I don't suppose there's any point asking if you are yourself again, since you seem to have some rather fundamental problems in that area. Isn't that true, Mr. Molberg? I mean, in terms of knowing who you are."

"Where am I?"

"You're in a suite. My suite."

"What happened?"

"You appeared to be very hungry," Jack Pascal says, fielding a smile from the man in the chair. "You came charging at me with a fork in your hand. It seems you were a bit too impatient to wait for an invitation to start eating."

"How long have I been out?"

"About an hour. We put a pretty effective drug in your drink, but not enough to kill you. However, since you seem to have a taste for it, we may give you the rest later."

He has changed into another shirt. There's no sign of dried blood on his chest. But he's the one. Jack Roth Pascal. He sits down on the couch opposite me: tall and dark, with very calm eyes. Because they're black, his eyes seem warm, but when he turns in the light, the pupils are small. His eyes are cold.

As he leans forward against the table, he pulls up his sleeves slightly. I see the scars on his hands.

"So, Mr. Molberg, what exactly is it you want?"

"I want her back."

"Do you really?"

"What's that supposed to mean?"

"I think you'd do yourself a favor if you accepted certain things."

"Such as?"

He gets up, walks over to the window and stands with his back turned to me.

"How would you describe your relationship to Monique? Was it—happy?"

"That's none of your business."

"Do you think Monique was happy? With you?"

"Of course she was."

"Then what was she doing with me?"

"I don't even know that she knew you."

"But what do you *think,* Mr. Molberg?"

"I don't know."

"There's a lot you don't know, Mr. Molberg. Monique knew that the greatest pleasure is inextricably connected to the greatest pain. Do *you* know that, Mr. Molberg? You haven't been able to figure that out, have you?"

"I have no idea what you're talking about."

"Don't you? Didn't you feel just the tiniest twinge of excitement when you saw her copulating with someone else in the photograph?"

I don't answer.

"That's your problem, Mr. Molberg. You can't live with it. It hurt you to see her lying there, but at the same time it excited you. Monique knew that. For her it wasn't a problem. It's the moment when we realize that we have what we can never own—namely each other—that we become liberated. Monique knew this, and she was able to live with it. But you can't."

"I don't have any idea what you're babbling about."

"Don't you, Mr. Molberg? Isn't the truth really that you *used* to love Monique? And that she changed? Isn't it true that she was actually about to leave you? And that you, in fact, didn't love her anymore?"

I look at him.

"Who's paying you to do this crap?"

He smiles.

"Do you expect me to answer that?"

"Isn't NSA paying your bill here?"

"Oh yes, that's right! Your little hotel spy! We were wondering how you knew where we were. That . . . upset things a bit."

"Upset what?"

He smiles, but doesn't answer.

"I work for a lot of different people, Mr. Molberg. For anyone who can pay. I like to think of myself as a kind of consultant. We're in a country that sets the pace. A country where it's necessary to explore all possibilities in the new technologies. I'm sure you're aware of the magnitude of the interests involved."

"In other words, you're blackmailing them. That's the way you work, isn't it?"

He looks at me with a guarded expression, as though something surprises him.

"Mr. Molberg, do you know why there are so many people out of work in the world? For some reason everyone seems to think that he needs to send an arsenal of personal information to his prospective employers. I've found the opposite to be far more effective."

"Did Monique work for you?"

"What do you think?"

"Perhaps. I don't know."

"What about the bank account? Didn't you suddenly come into money?"

"What do you know about the account?"

He turns his head away slightly. Maybe to hide a grimace.

"Was it you who deposited the money in the account, Mr. Pascal?"

He turns toward me, smiling. Then shakes his head. Slightly indulgently.

"To supply me with a motive?" I ask.

"You ask a lot of questions, Mr. Molberg."

"I'm a reporter."

He pauses, as if he's just remembered something. "That's right," he says, walking into the adjoining bedroom. He comes back with the tape recorder.

"This was in your pocket. You'd forgotten to turn it off. I've done it for you, so now we'll be able to speak more freely to each other, don't you agree?"

"I know what happened, Mr. Pascal."

He raises one eyebrow.

"Do you really, Mr. Molberg? Then tell me. By all means, tell me all about it."

"I think you got nervous the first time I checked into the hotel."

"Please continue, Mr. Molberg."

"You didn't know how much I knew. And you'd made a mistake about Monique. You'd thought you could intimidate her into silence. When you realized that you couldn't, you got worried that she might have let something slip. And you were worried about what she might have done with the video."

"The video?"

"I know there is a film. You showed it to her to make her behave, and you sent her a copy because you were so sure she'd come around. But she didn't! She kept the film, just the way she kept the photograph."

He listens attentively.

"It was you, not the police, who ransacked my apartment while I was here in LA. You were looking for the video, but you didn't find it. The film was dangerous. Nobody can really imagine the implications of digital TV, but if that film got out to the public, they might just catch on. And if that happened, then all the carefully planned preliminary work to develop the manipulation programs would have been wasted."

As I speak, I can hear how naive it all sounds. He laughs out loud.

"You don't seriously believe that one video is enough to stop the world from getting digital TV, do you, Mr. Molberg?"

"I don't know what I believe anymore."

He sucks at the end of a cigar, then leans forward in his chair. "Please continue, Mr. Molberg."

"When she saw the film, Monique got frightened. She panicked and tried to change her appearance. She cut her hair, but you just changed the hair in the film. Then you lifted a single frame out of the film and sent her the picture. After she received it, she dyed her hair. I have the photograph with her short, blond hair."

"And where exactly do you keep that photograph, Mr. Molberg?"

"In a safe place. In Copenhagen."

"And how did you get that photograph, Mr. Molberg?"

"Her girlfriend sent it to me."

He smiles. "Even for a reporter you're a lousy guesser," he says.

"Then explain it all to me."

"Why would I do that, Mr. Molberg? What makes you think that you can get answers to questions that no one else can? I know why you're here. Because you find it agonizing not to know, don't you? The uncertainty is the worst part. If you only knew what really happened. I'm not sure you even care what else is going to happen. So until then, I have you under my control. I have something you want, because I know what happened."

He lights his cigar, pulling at it calmly and slowly. Then puts out the match and drops the sooty, curled-up stick into the ashtray.

"Tell me something, Mr. Molberg. Why did you become a reporter?"

"Because I like to write."

He shakes his head.

"Because you like to look. You like staying at a distance from things, observing. You're a voyeur—just like everybody else. And what does everyone do about that small vice, which by definition is a perversion? They watch TV! Believe me, all the arguments in the world, however frightening, aren't going to stop us from getting digital television, interactive television. It's with us already, like a law of nature. And just think of the kind of experiences we can look forward to! Total surroundings that will ultimately be indistinguishable from the real thing. Soon we'll be able to add smells, tastes . . . and feelings.

"You're a reporter, Mr. Molberg. You don't seriously believe that things are going to get better? The population is growing and growing. What are all those people going to do? We have a responsibility to create a revolution in the only medium that can pacify all the masses. And believe me, Mr. Molberg, there'll be a lot of them."

"And all this is going on with the blessing of the American intelligence community—or whoever it is you're working for?"

"A few years ago, NSA . . . got wind . . . that a Danish company had made quite a bit of progress in a new animation program. A simple, clever program that solved some of the problems other programs were struggling with. Naturally, NSA can't officially enter into negotiations, so occasionally they contact independent experts."

"And exactly what do you have on NSA?"

"That's not the way we look at it, Mr. Molberg. If that term were ever used, I'd probably be a dead man. No, all we do is make deals, negotiate."

"And you do the same with DiaData?"

"We offered to buy the algorithms, but the company refused. In principle, we could have stolen most of it, but instead we offered to place some decoding keys into the company's external data communication system, which would secure it against other unwelcome guests. In principle the codes are unbreakable — some of the formulas are equivalent in length to the number of stars in the visible universe—but since it goes without saying that NSA doesn't care for unbreakable codes, naturally we're able to read along."

"In other words, DiaData develops, and you steal the results?"

"It's not that simple. As I said, we deal and negotiate. DiaData isn't the only company in the software race. Many of the best algorithms are to be found in the US, and I have . . . access . . . to quite a few of these companies. DiaData is an engine that's been tuned, while at the same time we've lowered its speed limit a little."

"And is a software program worth killing for?"

"You still don't understand, do you, Mr. Molberg? Just look at the alliances being made even as we speak: big and small, rivals and enemies are making deals, negotiating, all over the world. Telecommunication companies, media concerns, electronics companies, computer giants. Doesn't it make you stop and think? Don't you see what's happening? In five years we'll be talking about an industry dealing in trillion-dollar figures.

"And in terms of this particular product, the interested parties are climbing all over each other. You watched the Gulf War. Remember how easily the media allowed itself to be manipulated by the images that were made available to it? It wasn't always that way. And there will be other wars, but never another one lost because of a lack of the right images. That's the serious side of the coin, and this is where NSA's interests lie. The other side is the commercial one, the entertainment industry."

"Forgive me if I have trouble seeing the entertaining part."

"Do you really? Just try to imagine that you could have Monique back. Not the Monique we both know, but the one she was before. When you really did love her. Or what about your neighbor's wife? What about all your dirty little fantasies? And all the unattainable beauties in the world? It means the end of frustrated lusting after all of them. Digital images are the *ne plus ultra* of democracy. You can have them all, and any way you want them."

"You're sick."

"Possibly. But so are you. Because right now you're sitting there thinking it over."

"A sick swine."

"Swine? Are we the swine? Is it we, or is it all the people who feed on the worst perversions? Not many realize how big the porno market really is. Your own country is pretty skilled in the field. But then you practically invented the concept, didn't you?

"In the future there won't be any problems accommodating people's special wishes: showers of gold from Zeus, bestiality, spanking. The problem is that no one will admit to it. Don't you believe in free choice, Mr. Molberg? Who says people really want each other? Who says reality is good enough? We believe in a future of noninfectious, aesthetic sex, in which everything takes place anonymously and alone. That, Mr. Molberg, is the future."

"And Monique became a victim of your sick imagination?"

"I'm not exactly sure who she became a victim of."

"What do you mean?"

He bites his cigar lightly. Then calmly sucks the flame back into it.

"You've always had trouble with feelings, haven't you? I think Monique felt unappreciated. Unloved."

I don't answer.

He gets up and sits in a chair closer to me.

"Mr. Molberg, you've always been alone a lot, haven't you?"

I stare at him stiffly without answering.

"Do you realize that more than thirty-five percent of Danish households consist of single people like yourself?"

"I'm not alone."

He takes the cigar out of his mouth. Picks at a leaf in his mouth and chews it a little.

"Now you are."

I'm about to pounce, but stay on the couch.

"What did you do to her?"

"What did I do?" He gets up and walks over to the open balcony door. "Why don't you ask what she did to me?" He turns. "Do you realize, Mr. Molberg, that oral sex is still illegal in several American states?"

"You're full of shit!"

"Am I? Do you want to see pictures?"

"I can't trust your pictures."

"I thought you wanted to know what happened, but now you don't seem to after all."

"Did she smuggle for you?"

"Oh, you want the nice details. I should've known. You're such a nice young man. Yes, she did."

"I don't understand how you got her to do it."

"Which answer do you want, Mr. Molberg? The truth, or one of the many other alternative answers? You don't know yourself, do you? You don't know what you want. But I'll give you the nice version. There's something about women and technology— and this may sound chauvinistic to your Scandinavian ears—that just doesn't mesh. I told Monique what she was carrying around, but do you know, Mr. Molberg, she didn't care."

"But did you have to kill her? I don't get it!"

"Don't you, Mr. Molberg? Is that really true? What makes you think that we're looking for that all-important film? What makes you think that we don't already have it?"

I look at him.

"That's impossible. It was at her friend's house, and now it's gone."

"Is it, Mr. Molberg? Don't you wonder about the break-in at your apartment? Haven't you wondered how we got in?"

Of course I've wondered, but I've lied to myself. Only in crime movies do all the clues lead to something. In reality you can never be sure what happened; you can only trust your instincts, and they're either right or dead wrong. I thought there were other possibilities. But actually there was only one.

"Marianne."

He shrugs.

"If you have enough money, Mr. Molberg, you'd be surprised what you can buy."

"I don't believe you."

He snaps his fingers, and the bodyguard walks up to the cabinet and takes out a video.

"Wouldn't you like to see the film? Then you'll be able to decide if it's real or not."

I consider it for a moment.

"But I know it isn't."

"Do you, Mr. Molberg? Do you really?"

Obviously Monique didn't bring her keys when she left that last day. Why should she? She wasn't heading home. She just left her keys at her best friend's house, where she was living. Klinker did ask me a few times about the keys. Did I think she might have thrown them away? I answered that she might have. But of course she didn't.

Marianne sent me the photograph. The conversations with her. They've had the key the whole time. Everything is churning around in my brain.

"But if Marianne had the film, what was she searching for in my apartment?"

"Knowledge, Mr. Molberg, knowledge. We weren't sure if Monique had made a copy of the film. This is a converted PAL copy. But now we know that she didn't, and we also know that she didn't write down anything too incriminating."

"But if that's true, then that means that . . ."

"Quite right, Mr. Molberg, we've been waiting for you. And in a way we still are. Now I'm sure that even you can figure out the rest."

I can. I see it. I've walked straight into a trap that was set a long time ago. Starting with the photograph sent by Marianne, to Natasha in Los Angeles. I've been shadowed the whole time. Not by the police, but by them. There's been a plan all along, a program, which they've been following systematically, and still are. Monique's murder. Kubjec's murder. What's missing is a suspect.

"What about Kubjec? What did he have to do with all this?"

He smiles pensively.

"You'll probably remember that for a period of time several years ago, military doctors were experimenting with LSD and other psychoactive drugs, using young American soldiers as volunteers."

I nod.

"Kubjec was also a kind of guinea pig. Are you familiar with sensory simulation?"

"Artificial reality? Virtual reality?"

He nods.

"Kubjec was involved in a series of experiments. The reason for these particular experiments was an accident that occurred during the Gulf War. A pilot dropped his bombs far from the designated target. It didn't cause a major catastrophe, but of course it did give rise to concern, because it turned out that the pilot, who—like every other pilot—had been trained in simulators, had had an 'attack' in the middle of his mission. An attack which to a frightening degree was reminiscent of the relapses experienced by many LSD patients. A flashback, the so-called trigger effect, when the artificial reality suddenly becomes real again, but in the real world. Kubjec had the same experience."

He shows me his hands.

"I was in a car with him. Suddenly he was back in the simulator. He lost control of the car, and we just barely got out of it before it exploded."

"Touching."

He looks at me, annoyed, as if he regrets having said something that sounds intimate.

"Why did you kill him?" I say.

"We had to. He became . . . unstable." He leans back in his chair. "What if I told you that it was Kubjec who met Monique in the basement, and that he went berserk. That he had one of his attacks. That the whole thing was an accident?"

"What was she doing in the basement?"

"We'd asked her to bring the film and the photograph. We felt they belonged to us. I'm sure you understand how important the photograph and film were to us. Since she didn't bring them, Kubjec went . . . a little crazy. It wasn't supposed to happen."

I look at him skeptically.

"You don't seriously expect me to believe this?"

He grins.

"No, it's got to be me, doesn't it, Mr. Molberg? You really have it in for me. But what kind of case do you really have? As far as I understand, you've got some rather substantial problems with the Danish police at the moment. If I came forth and said that Kubjec did it, then everything would be solved. I'd promise to produce several witnesses who'd be willing to swear that they'd heard him openly blame himself for what he'd done, and that he was planning to take his own life."

"Kubjec wasn't there. You were. You killed her."

"But you don't *know* that, Mr. Molberg. You don't know anything for sure. In fact it could have been anybody. It doesn't have to be anything as extreme as simulators and drugs that cause blackouts. It can be jealousy, pills, alcohol. In fact, you yourself might have done it."

"I wasn't there," I say.

"No, but no one else knows that, Mr. Molberg. Kubjec was your witness. Now he's dead."

Starting to stand up, he gestures to one of his bodyguards and whispers something in his ear.

"Tell me one thing, Pascal: what's the point of this whole production?"

"We have our sponsors, Mr. Molberg. We have resources, but they're not unlimited. There are people who want to see artificial reality tested on the real one. There are people who want to be convinced."

"So it's supposed to look like I killed them?" I say.

"That's what it does look like."

"What'll happen now?" I say.

He looks at me and smiles. A psychotic smile.

"Figure it out! Figure it out, Mr. Molberg. I've just made you an offer, and you've rejected it."

I have no idea how many hours I have left of my life. How many minutes. Maybe we're talking about seconds. Somehow I have to get to the tear-gas capsule in my cigarette pack.

"Would it be all right if I smoked a cigarette?" I say.

Jack Pascal looks at me. Then nods at the man sitting next to me.

"Give him a cigarette."

I curse quietly to myself.

As calmly as possible I take the cigarette. Then I hold it and study it carefully.

"If you don't mind terribly, I'd prefer one of my own."

I place a hand on my pocket, then look up at each one of them, expectantly. No one protests and Jack Pascal nods approvingly.

I rip it open, jamming my finger against the tip of the capsule. A fat, intense cloud of gas spurts into the room. As long as I can, I hold the capsule directly at his face; he's about to suffocate when one of his bodyguards attacks. I drag myself toward the door, pulling the bodyguard along; my throat feels like it's being ripped open. Pascal and the other guard instinctively flee toward the open balcony. I keep beating at the man who's locked himself around my leg, and just as I reach the door, I feel his grip loosen. I'm about to collapse in the suffocating stench, but I get the door open. And start running.

Chapter Nineteen

Jan Borris is one of the first people I run into after I finally manage to convince the guards to let me into the pool party.

"Well, have you sobered up?" he says, scrutinizing me closely. I'm breathing heavily, my whole body aches, and I'm sweating.

"You look like shit," he says.

Women in dresses and men in tuxedos encircle the pool. It's dark now. In the middle of the crowd, the center of attention is Jack Nicholson, surrounded by the obligatory guards. The mood is high. Some jackets and ties have already been shed, and out over the city of millions, a myriad of lights flicker from windows and from the planes approaching LAX. Among the skyscrapers downtown hover police helicopters.

I try to catch my breath. Sweat pours out of my hair and runs down my face.

"Jan, I need your help. They're after me."

"Who? Your creditors?"

At that moment Pascal and his friends appear at the entrance. The guards point; they see me.

There's no way out. The elevator to the restaurant is blocked by a bar table. I could leap over the wall on the other side of the pool, but there's a four-story drop. I can't take the stairs to the deck where there's usually a barbecue, because the stairs too are blocked for the evening's affair. There is no way out.

"Jan, this is serious. You're the only one I know here. I'm in major trouble."

He laughs and pushes me away.

"I can't imagine how you got in, and I don't care. I don't know you, pal," he says, grinning. "Why don't you ask your good friend Nicholson to help you?"

He walks away.

Calmly but quickly, Pascal and one of his bodyguards are making their way toward me.

I walk over toward Jack Nicholson and exclaim:

"Jack! How nice to see you again!"

Silence. Heads turn, the guards turn, and from within his cluster of bodyguards, the little man turns his face.

I smile broadly and glance back at my pursuers.

"Don't you remember me? At the pool?"

If I'm convincing, I have a chance, so I'm loud. I can't see his reaction—even in the evening he's wearing sunglasses. But he's not smiling.

The guards watch him expectantly. By now the party is completely quiet. Nicholson himself seems to be in doubt. Then he opens his arms and smiles.

"Fans! Can't even keep 'em out of the cabanas," he says indulgently. Then turns his back. I can see Borris shaking his head. Scattered laughter ripples through the party.

A few of Mr. Nicholson's guards close in to form a tighter

circle around him. The little scene has caught the attention of the door guards. One of them is walking toward Pascal and his bodyguard, who are on their way toward me.

Now there's only one way out.

The bar table blocking the exit to the restaurant is under an awning, and a little half-roof juts out above it. As I run, Pascal's bodyguard takes a swing at me, knocks me into the guests jammed around the bar. But I jump onto the table, sliding around in the spills, catch the edge of the overhang, and pull myself up. A hush goes through the crowd as I run across the half-roof. "Stop him!" someone shouts. They're right behind me.

I jump to the next overhang and the next, then stand and stare at the hotel entrance five stories down. I'm right below the corner balcony of the lowest room facing the pool. There's no light inside—probably no one's there—so I grab the lower edge of the balcony and pull myself up. Just as I land, light comes on inside the room and one of Pascal's bodyguards runs toward the door. I climb over the railing and jump to the next level, out of his reach. This room is lit, so I crawl sideways from one balcony to another all the way to the hotel facade facing the street. There are only about three feet between these balconies, so it's easier to move in this direction. Glancing down into the abyss now and then, I keep crawling, then stop to orient myself. At some point I've got to go through one of the rooms, but as I look up, down, to one side, to the other, one of the bodyguards leaps at me from inside a room. As I throw myself over the railing of the next balcony, I don't see him fall, but I do hear the thump as he bounces on the awning of the hotel entrance far below. He doesn't move. He lies sprawled on the pavement. To confuse them and win time, I climb onto the railing and try to jump to the next floor, but I jump too high and my hands hit the railing instead of the ledge. I realize that there's hardly any strength left in my arms. I manage to pull myself halfway up, and I see that the room is dark. I decide to go in.

At that moment I feel a weight on my leg. It's Pascal. He's balancing on the railing of the balcony below me. I kick out at him, but as he lets go, he leaps up beside me on the ledge. Flinging his legs around me, he tries to pull me loose and down, but I hold on to the railing with one hand and with the other pound his head as if my fist were a hammer. My legs are free now; I fling one over the railing, and pull myself up. I try the door. Locked. He's close behind me.

He seems to be enjoying himself. Grinning and out of breath, he's struggling on to the balcony.

"Why not let bygones be bygones?" he says. He has his elbows on the edge of the railing.

"All young girls dream of becoming movie stars. It just happened that Monique made it," he says, grinning. "Let's put it all behind us, Mr. Molberg. Don't you believe in happy endings?"

"No!" I say, kicking with all my might as he tries to throw his leg over the edge. I see his hands clawing at the air, then he's gone. Both hands disappear as he falls.

I don't wait for the sound. I back up and cover my face with my jacket. Just before crashing through the glass, I see a hand on the railing; it must be the other bodyguard. In a rain of splintered glass I land inside the room. I look back: no one's there now. I walk through the dark room to the door and open it a crack. No one.

On the other side of the hall I knock on several doors. No answer. The hall's quiet. I try forcing a door, but it's impossible. I try the next. Still no answer. Finally a young Japanese woman opens the third door a crack. I kick it the rest of the way.

Apologizing profusely, throwing money on her bed, I rush through the room to her open balcony door.

"I won't hurt you. I just need to get downstairs. Don't worry. And don't tell anyone."

She doesn't nod. She doesn't smile. She's scared to death.

"I promise I won't hurt you. Please don't say a word."

She nods, confused.

I crawl from her balcony to the next. All the rooms on this level are dark. I crawl all the way to the last one. I look back. The Japanese woman is watching me from her balcony. At least this is giving me some time. At the end of the row of rooms, I climb over the railing and jump down to the next level, then continue down until I'm on the first floor. From there I leap into something that looks like a soft, exotic bush. Surprisingly, its strong branches flip me into the air and dump me at street level with a whack. I limp out to the street at the back of the hotel: not a soul around. As best I can, I run down a side street toward Beverly Center. Then cross over to the first side street, take the first right, the next left, until I end up on Sunset Boulevard.

By Samuel French's music store, I hail a cab.

"Where to, sir?"

"San Francisco."

Chapter Twenty

The flight:

I sleep most of the way home. A flight attendant wakes me up.

"Don't you want to see the movie?"

"Who's in it?"

"Meg Ryan."

"Are you sure?"

At Copenhagen Central Station I walk past the parked cars and stand for a while staring down into the pit where trains snake along the tracks: the soft silver entrails of the big city. Behind the trains, dead leaves are churned up in clouds, like loose dirt behind the paws of wild dogs. Far off on the horizon, glinting whitely, a plane is pushing its way into the sky. A flock of pigeons rises in a confused cascade and glides off on beating wings.

They'll find me soon. They'll make a connection between the murder in Los Angeles and Martin Molberg the reporter who was in Los Angeles at the exact time of the murder. The hotel will confirm it. Before I left LA, I checked the TV news, but there was nothing yet. I was sure I'd be stopped in the airport, but I went right through the gate. Nothing happened.

I imagine that people are staring at me, but that may be because my eyes look like two tomatoes and my face is as white as a death mask.

Underneath my clothes my body is covered with multicolored bruises that change like the seasons from blue to purple to black to a sickly yellow, before they finally fade like shadows on the skin.

As I drift aimlessly through the streets, I keep checking behind me. Dr. Phillip would express concern about my paranoid behavior.

I avoid my apartment. I don't know if it's safe. This is the city where I was born. Its rhythms have always been a part of me. Now I don't know where to go.

I head for the harbor, I drift up and down along the piers, but it feels empty. White sails flapping, sailboats are moving through the Sound. There are still families—yelping puppies, young girls, wet kisses, long rainy days, fog, silhouettes of blue forests, summerhouses, campfire nights, songs, secrets, light, happiness, life. But more and more, people need to remind themselves that they exist.

I pace the wharf like a caged animal. I've killed two people, but I feel nothing. No anger, no guilt. Monique and I used to take long walks together here. Maybe I brought something out in Monique. The something I did not like in myself.

I return to the Central Station, go to the departure hall, and call Marianne. No answer. So I go to see her.

The suburbs rush past the windows of the train. Film clips in a montage: a dog on a lawn, tail wagging, chasing a stick. The Danish flag flapping on a garden flagpole. Denmark, islands of green beech trees. It's been this way for a thousand years, lying underneath a chaotic sky—drifting, ragged clouds in the west and a churning rumble in the northeast. Denmark. The way it's always been. I feel nothing: no sadness, no melancholy, no joy.

We're on our way to another world. A new millennium. But we can't see it. It's sneaking up on us imperceptibly. We don't protest because we don't notice, and we don't notice because we don't protest. We simply pay no attention anymore, not to anything. Not serious attention. We let ourselves be anesthetized in front of the evening's images. Brain-dead narcissists lead us through idiotic television games, news programs bring us to war zones with images of the wounded and mutilated, but the only thing that bothers us is that no one dies when we press the remote. But that'll come, too. It's on its way.

One by one, without causing much of a stir, the prophesies of the past are coming true before the eyes of a public that has always reminded itself of the importance of learning from the past. By not protesting, we're passively accepting fines as sufficient punishment for polluters who have destroyed yet another piece of our planet. The currency crises of other countries placate us, for we can always cite a statistic that makes us feel that we're not doing as badly as someone else. We live a godless existence with our new god. We're the ones who decide how wise it can get. So far. And yet we're at its mercy. It eliminates one job after another, and still we praise it. "We" are the ones who control it; "they" are the opportunists. The power brokers. Everyone else is lost. We simply don't give a damn anymore.

The house, a pale apricot-painted home with elegant, small-paned windows, sits on a quiet side street. One summer two years ago, we went to a party here. When Monique was still alive.

A car is parked on the sidewalk in front of the house, and the wind makes ocean sounds in the large birch in the front garden. In the backyard a few cypresses tower above the house like Greek columns, and even though it's a windy day, they seem fossilized.

I consider ringing the doorbell, but decide to wait a while. I pass by the house a few times, but there's no sign of life. Aimlessly I drift around the neighborhood. Time creeps by.

On the horizon, clouds have started to gather into a wide blue-black belt. Distant thunder. Soon it'll start to rain.

I return to the house. Still no one there. Then suddenly the door opens, and a young man steps out onto the stairs.

"Looking for someone?"

"Marianne," I say. "The woman who lives here."

"She's gone," he says. Then he walks toward me down the garden path.

He smiles a friendly smile when he gets to the gate.

"I saw you nosing around. We're new here. We just bought the house."

"Do you know where she went?"

"South America, she said. It all happened so quickly. We closed on the house just a couple of weeks ago. We got it for a hundred thousand below the appraisal."

"When did she leave?"

"Yesterday, I think. Do you know her?"

"Not as well as I thought I did."

It's pouring. The train snakes its way through a landscape dark with rain. It's late afternoon, but the rain makes it feel like night. Of course she's gone. She'll never come back. Pascal is right:

everything can be bought for money. Everything except what we've lost.

At the Central Station I go back to the telephone booths in the departure hall. I call the airport and ask for Marianne.

"Marianne Nordentoft. Just a moment. She's in Buenos Aires. She'll be back in three weeks."

"Not likely."

"Excuse me, who am I speaking to?"

I hang up.

Then I call Lindvig.

"They're looking for you. The police have been here asking for you."

"I think I killed him."

He's silent for a moment, then he says:

"Martin, you can stay here, but I don't think it's safe. They'll probably be back."

"I don't know what to do."

"Leave! Go to another country!"

"That's not what I mean. I don't know what to do now."

He doesn't know what to say. There's nothing he can say. What do you say to someone who has nothing more to do? Nothing. There is nothing to say.

Only when the night is completely dark do I dare go near my apartment. I walk all the way. The rain's beating down on everything. Parked cars, thick foliage, houses. It spurts and sprays in the headlight beams from the occasional car creeping through the streets.

If I still have the photograph, I may have a chance. Lindvig will back me up. Maybe Stig Plaun too.

Soaked to the skin, I turn the corner of my street. A car blinks nervously as it pulls up next to the jeweler's; maybe it's got a twitch in the wiring. The rain drums on the car roof. Everything's rusting.

Then I stop. I can still turn back. I can put everything behind me, and walk the other way. I can start from scratch. I can go directly to the airport, buy a ticket to some other country. Just like Marianne. But it's no good. Something is driving me forward. Maybe it's the need for an ending. Everything has a beginning, middle, and end. This has to have an ending.

The rain pours down on the deserted street and parked cars. Like heavy, shiny curtains, the tarps hang at the end of the street opposite my building. From time to time the wind lifts them and beats them heavily against the scaffolding. Closer by, in the young woman's apartment, there's light. She was a bit player in a drama she probably doesn't give a thought to anymore. Maybe she's met someone. Maybe the police are there right now. She never used to keep on so many lights. In the row of bay windows, which jut out like kneecaps from the building on my side of the street, all the windows are lit except mine and Zenia's on the top floor. Maybe they're sitting in the dark, waiting.

From the streetlights between the trees a faint, ghostly light flutters here and there from the wind and rain.

I walk slowly down the street.

As I get to the entrance, I hesitate. Everything seems peaceful, but I continue on, turning the corner to the back gate, and let myself in. The yard is dark. Water drips from the garbage cans and gurgles into the drains. Nothing else. No sign of life from the apartment.

I cross the backyard and let myself in by the back stairs. When

I pull the wooden door open too hard, the chain rattles loudly. I grab it. Silence.

Slowly, without making a sound, I walk up the narrow, winding stairs. Hesitating outside my apartment, I carefully put my ear to the door and listen. There's nothing to hear, so I unlock the door, turning the key carefully, as if the door were a safe. In the kitchen I stand still for a few seconds, listening. All is quiet.

Then I crawl along the kitchen floor into the hall, expecting the lights to come on at any moment. Nothing happens. I continue along the hallway molding. The slanted venetian blinds in the living room let in narrow strips of light that run along the ceiling. No one but me is in the room. When I reach the couch, I get up on one knee and push my hand under the seat cushion. The photograph is there. I have a chance.

The phone rings.

My heart is beating loudly in my head; it's almost impossible for me not to answer. When the phone rings again, it feels like it's threatening to alert the whole building. I sit in front of it as the answering machine kicks in.

"Martin! Martin, are you there?"

It sounds as if she's right in the apartment, calling for me. Natasha.

"Martin, if you're there, please answer!" She pauses. I can hear the room behind her like a buzz. She rattles the receiver. Then she's back:

"I think . . . wait a second . . ."

"Natasha!" I call. "Natasha!" But she's put down the receiver. Maybe because of the darkness, I can practically see her walking around her apartment. I hear scratching and scraping behind her, as if someone's trying to get in. Suddenly there's a loud, ripping sound, like wood being cracked open. Then footsteps across the floor, and her voice. Closer:

"Oh, God! Oh, no! Not that . . ."

"Natasha!"

Then the scream. Noise. Crashing sounds. Finally the dial tone when the connection is broken.

I put the photograph back under the seat cushion. Then I start running. Everything turns into speed: I tear open the door, slipping in my wet shoes, leap down the stairs, kick open the outside door, into the car, start, back it up, wheels spinning, left turn, accelerate, then slow down, left turn, accelerate, wheels spinning in second gear, splashing through puddles, traffic lights green, yellow, yellow, top speed, the next intersection, yellow, yellow, yellow, red, honking the horn, across Åboulevarden, slipping and slaloming my way among the cars of Bispeengbuen down Borup's Allé. Only then does it dawn on me that I won't make it in time.

Before I know it, I'm in front of her building. I run up to the door. All seems dead. Push all the buzzers. No response. I curse loudly.

"I don't believe this."

"Yes?" an old voice says. An old, cracked woman's voice.

"Open the door!" I shout. "Let me in!"

"Who is it?"

"It's for Natasha. It's important."

"Well then, she's going to have to let you in herself. I can't just let . . ."

"Open the goddamn door!"

"Certainly not! Who do you think . . ."

"Forget it."

". . . you are? Just coming and . . ."

I run around the building to the back entrance. Climb over the fence and land on the other side in the backyard. Across the roof of a bicycle shed. The door to the back stairs is wide open.

I run up to the fourth floor. The door is open: looks like it was broken down with an ax.

She's lying in the living room.

Dripping.

Half her face is covered with blood. At first I think she's alive because blood is still pumping out of her stomach. The couch she's leaning against has been pushed askew, and the floor looks as if it's been swept with red, liquid roses. I grab the back of her neck. It's like holding warm porridge. I put her back down gently. Her eyes are staring stiffly at the ceiling.

There's a knock at the door. "Open up!"

I have to let it sink in. Confused, I stare around the room. The pickax is lying on the coffee table, and on the harpsichord is a kitchen knife covered with blood. My knife. For a split second I imagine the feel of the fillet knife blade slicing into flesh.

As the noise from the hallway increases, I begin to understand that it must be the police. Only then do I wake up. Only then do I realize my situation.

With a mixture of fear and shock I throw up on the floor. I try holding in the vomit with my hands. But it pours out of me.

Then I run down the back stairs again and out into the street. By the inside wall before the street I try to pull myself together. A police car is parked behind mine. It's empty. They must both be upstairs at the door. I'm about to run up to my car when a woman comes toward me on the sidewalk.

"Molberg? Martin Molberg?"

I go to her.

"Yes," I say.

Time has erased most of the similarities, but there's still something of Natasha in her features. She stands holding an umbrella behind her. Like an old woman with her shawl.

"You were the one who called me that night, weren't you?"

I nod. Water is running down my face from my hair. Maybe the rain will remove the mixture of vomit and blood on my hands. Maybe she won't see it.

"What did you do to her? What are the police doing here?"

I don't know what to say.

"I'm afraid there's been a misunderstanding."

"Why do you do these things?"

"It's not me who's doing it. It's very hard to explain, but . . ."

"Just because you have a lot of money, that doesn't give you the right to . . . do you think that . . . ?"

Her voice breaks. Tears well up in her eyes. She clears her throat and bites her lip.

"How do you think it feels to be called by your daughter . . . and then?" She collects herself. "How badly did you beat her?"

"Are you sure it was Natasha who called you?"

She notices my hands. I shake them a little farther up into my sleeves.

She looks at me, enraged.

"You filthy pig!"

She strides by me, and I have to move to avoid being poked in the face by her umbrella.

"Mrs. Noiret! Don't go up there . . ."

She stops and turns around.

"If something's happened to her, I know who you are, Martin Molberg. I just pray that she's all right."

"Mona!"

She stops.

"Don't go up there . . . !"

Suddenly the street is full of police cars. The blue lights flash on the faces of the officers. At first I walk calmly toward my car. Then I start to run. Just as I'm about to open the door, someone hits my arm and I'm crushed against the car door.

"Back in my apartment there's a photograph in the couch. And there's a tape on the answering machine . . ."

They're on top of me. Pushing me down onto the wet grass next to the sidewalk, they push my face into the muddy lawn.

"Just take it easy!"

I manage to squeeze out:

"It's important!"

"Just take it easy."

Chapter Twenty-One

If you could define meaning. And then forget the process. If you could scream out loudly or smash a window. And then be able to think the glass whole again.

We lose everything when we lose something precious. When we experience loss for the first time. We stop caring. We lower our demands and standards and tell ourselves that we're growing up—when the truth is that we're slowly getting ready to be corrupted forever.

We're not moved by the diminishing oxygen in the ocean because we've forgotten the feel of sand and seaweed under our toes. Atomic waste forces itself up from underground in the East, like radioactive mushrooms, while the international narcotics cartels infiltrating all levels of government merely confirm an old prejudice—that all Italians are crooks. The only audible comment on the famines in Africa are if we happen to belch after a hastily consumed meal while TV images glide across the screen. Worst of all, we contradict ourselves, claiming absolute control while cynically admitting that the extinction of the human race should come as no surprise in a world where one species after another is continually being eliminated. We admit our guilt in the process but not in the act itself, and thereby we talk ourselves into believing that we've been granted absolution. Something is making me see all this clearly. Maybe I'm catatonic.

There are interrogations: endlessly long, exhausting interrogations.

Fall is coming. The elm leaves are turning yellow and crumbling like paper that catches fire; the shadows along the street below turn long. Low sun.

Dr. Phillip sits on the windowsill holding his papers.

He asks how I'm feeling.

"A bit of a headache," I say.

He starts tapping.

"It'll pass."

He takes off his glasses and rubs his eyes. The frame has dug a reddish groove on the bridge of his nose.

Dr. Phillip and his idiotic tests:

"Hearts?"

"Death."

"Childhood?"

"Crime."

"Folded hands?"

"Spiders fighting. One of them dies."

He gathers up his papers, then goes over and speaks quietly to the physician in charge. Soon they walk out, saying nothing.

They don't know what to do with me. Occasionally their doubt makes them plug me into electrical circuits.

I stand by the window. Behind the pane.

A fiery yet fading golden light filters through the tree crowns almost enveloping in flames the beautiful women who speed in and out of the shops. All these women with dramatically colored eyes and mohair sweaters with soft nuances, ragged and fluffy like the pelts of aging jungle animals.

Inspector Klinker comes to visit. He drills me again. Asks me the same questions:

"Why did you come up the back stairs?"

"I told you already. The old lady refused to let me in. Didn't you talk to her?"

He nods.

"What did she say? Does she remember me?"

"Yes, but she doesn't remember if it was before or after she heard noises. You might have run out of the apartment and back down to the front door after the murder."

"What does Natasha's mother say?"

"That you had blood on your hands."

"Who called her?"

"Natasha. She was frightened. She said you were beating her. She called while you were in the bathroom. She asked her mother to come as quickly as possible."

"Is she sure it was Natasha who called?"

He looks at me quizzically.

"What do you mean?"

"You really don't see it, do you, Klinker?"

"See what?"

"That it was all planned. That there's a whole organization be-hind it." As I say it, I know how insane it sounds. Every word I say only makes my situation worse.

He gets up.

"This 'organization' had to mobilize quite an operation just to get at you."

"But that's just the point."

He looks like one large question mark.

"To show that it's possible."

"I'm not really sure where you're going with this, Molberg. We have three bodies, and you knew all three of them."

"What about the bodies in Los Angeles?"

"There are no bodies in Los Angeles. At least not the ones you're talking about. Try to concentrate, Molberg. If the answering machine tape turns out to be genuine, it won't necessarily give you an alibi. It might have been made at another time; we can't determine that. But since it's the only thing you have going for you, try to tell me what was on it."

"She says my name. She thinks I'm in the apartment. Then she says: 'Wait a moment.' Then I hear noises in the background. It sounds as if someone's trying to break in through the back door . . . I shout . . . I shout her name."

"Why do you think it's the back door?"

"The front door is heavier. It would have sounded different."

"Hmm," he says. "It's interesting that you're so focused on the sound."

"Why is that?"

"Because it means that you actually believe that you heard that conversation on the telephone."

"What do you mean, *believe*?"

"Just what I'm saying," he says, taking a tape recorder out of his pocket. He looks at me expectantly.

"Can you stand hearing it again?" he says. I nod. He pushes the button. The tape hisses, and it keeps on hissing.

"You probably need to rewind it."

"It was rewound. This is the beginning. But it doesn't change, Molberg. There's nothing on the tape."

"Let me see it."

He pushes the tape out of the machine and hands it to me.

I study it.

"That's not the tape that was in the machine."

"It is the tape that we found there."

"They've exchanged it."

He looks at me resignedly. Then gets up.

"Hold on to the thing about the sound. You'll have no problem claiming temporary insanity. You really are sick, Molberg. Very sick."

He walks to the door.

"What about the photograph? Didn't you find the photograph either?"

He smiles.

"Yes, and we even found the negative in the envelopes."

"Which photo was it? Didn't you speak to Lindvig?"

"Yes, we did, Molberg. He's a close friend of yours, isn't he? But we're talking about the photograph you say you put under the cushion, right?"

"Yes."

"Then that's the one. It was under a cushion in the couch."

"Did you check the background of the picture?"

"Yes we did. It was taken in your apartment one summer, a couple of years ago."

"It's not the right photograph! They changed it!"

"We took the one under the cushion," he says dryly. Then he looks at me, shaking his head. "How could anyone kill such a beautiful woman?"

"I didn't kill her."

"Molberg, you killed your fiancée. And you killed Kubjec. Sooner or later we'll find out why. He probably wouldn't cover you with his phony story anymore. There are some odd financial aspects . . . some odd transactions between his and your accounts. But you know all about that. We'll figure it out, Molberg. We'll figure it all out."

"Kubjec took the pictures of me. He filmed me. They needed the movements. They can't do it without the movements."

"What are you talking about?"

I collapse.

"Nothing. It doesn't matter anymore," I say.

He grips the doorjamb as though he's about to leave.

"What about Natasha?" I ask.

"We're searching for the gloves you must have used. We already have the knife. When we find your gloves, we'll have the final piece of evidence."

He remains in the doorway. Then he says thoughtfully:

"Dr. Phillip tells me that for you everything you say that's happened seems completely real. That you experience it just as authentically as I experience this conversation. But when we find the gloves, there won't be any doubt. Not for any of us."

Evening. It's windy. The city's asleep.

Somewhere out there she lay in the arms of a stranger. Maybe I was replaced by someone else. Maybe permanently.

Did they also lie together like spoons, or did she sit on him spread-eagled, and did she put his member inside her with her hand and let him empty himself in her? Did she walk on his feet with her arms thrown around his neck, and did they sit at night drinking tea as she held the mug with her little-mitten grip, making him gush with tenderness at the sight? Did they have their own intimate universe of words and sounds, and was it exactly like what we had? Did I look exactly like him? I don't think so, and that's what scares me.

It could have been Monique and I lying there, but it wasn't. It was someone else, a stranger, and that is meaningless.

Only when you discover how accidental everything is do you begin to fear chance. When I was young, chance had a patina of magic. Its principles were very close to the comforting thoughts of fate. In the flush of youth, accidental meetings looked very like clean-cut decisions from the guiding hand of God.

It's completely dark now.

A storm is raging outside. Tearing leaves from the trees. Rain whips through the streets. Creating a gruel of leaves on the sidewalk. There's still scattered light in some windows. Here and there blue light from the television screens.

They sit there night after night, hand in hand, as if in front of a common enemy. Sometimes the images may give them a sense of liberation, as when a symbiosis occurs between nonreflecting TV screens and nonreflecting thoughts, for if the illusion that images create is completely successful, its contours are farther-reaching than thought itself.

Night after night they sit there, just like people before them sat when the world was still young, hand in hand, night after night, waiting in helpless terror for the Great White Light: when the image exploded into flickering spots, or perhaps when death entered. Like an electric storm. Night after night they sit there now, but the signal will never stop or be changed to snow-white flickers. Never again will they be reminded that darkness is falling and day is ending. One day, sometime in the future,

Monique will appear on their screens. In ribbons of color and shapes created from numbers.

It happened out there. Maybe everything has closed up again, as water closes over itself after the splash of a rock. The crime took place out there. Maybe all traces have been removed. But now there's a piece missing. Maybe it was just in the way.

Or maybe I'm exaggerating everything. Maybe Jack Roth Pascal is right. Maybe everything will be better. In the future. Maybe we just need to adjust to it. Give in. We've lost so much along the way anyway, that maybe we'll be free only when we lose everything. When we surrender ourselves to the artificial world that's already a part of us. Maybe it's the resistance that hurts. One solution is to give in, go with the flow, let things happen. If it won't make us happy, maybe it'll make us less unhappy. And maybe that amounts to the same thing. We may not even notice that we've changed; we won't be able to sense the tough skin of others because we'll have it ourselves. Maybe he's right. Love lived with Monique. But maybe not until it died.

Days pass. I don't know how many. I can't keep track of them anymore. There are day-long therapeutic sessions, and increasing worry and concern because the confession or breakdown fails to come.

One evening the nurse enters.

"There's a phone call for you."

I go to my room and pick up the receiver. It's silent for a while, then I hear the voice:

"You're a reporter, Mr. Molberg. Don't forget to watch the news."

I answer tonelessly:

"I saw you falling . . ."

There's a short pause, then he says:

"Don't believe everything you see."

He hangs up.

An attendant rushes in.

"Mr. Molberg, the news is on."

"Yes."

He stands there fidgeting.

"You're on it."

"Yes."

I can hear bits and pieces of what the announcer is saying. "The news . . . has just come into our possession . . . videotapes . . . Tom Kubjec . . . reporter Martin Molberg . . . accused of . . . several murders . . . video amateur . . . sensational footage . . . from the apartment . . . the murder of Monique Milazar . . . Natasha Noiret . . . gas explosion . . . blackmail . . . witness . . . Kubjec may have been killed too . . . we now show . . . send out a warning . . ."

The attendant looks at me, horrified. I stand, silently watching the images. It's as if I've been there. As if it's me.

Then I walk past the attendant, who steps aside. I go back to my bed. Lie down. Pull the down comforter up around my body. It feels good. It's as taut as a coffin of soft down. It might have been me. It looked like me. So maybe it was me. I can't tell the difference anymore.

Between anything at all.

© Gregers Nielson

ABOUT THE AUTHOR

MICHAEL LARSEN was born in 1961 in Copenhagen. *Uncertainty* is his first novel to be translated into English.